The New World

Sunsinger Books

Illinois Short Fiction

THE NEW WORLD
Tales by Russell Banks

UNIVERSITY OF ILLINOIS PRESS

Urbana and Chicago

The author would like to thank the John Simon Guggenheim
Foundation, whose generous support helped make it possible to
bring this book to completion.

"The Custodian" first appeared in the *New Boston Review.*
"The Perfect Couple," *Fiction International,* nos. 6/7 (1976).
"About the Late Zimma (Penny) Cate," *TriQuarterly,* Fall, 1977.
"The Conversion," *Shenandoah,* Fall, 1977.
"The Rise of the Middle Class," *Canto,* September, 1977.
"Indisposed," *Matrix,* June, 1978.
"The Caul," *Mississippi Review,* Spring, 1978.
"The Adjutant Bird," *Lillabulero* 1, no. 3 (July, 1967).
"The New World," *Ploughshares* 3, no. 2 (1976).

Library of Congress Cataloging-in-Publication Data
Banks, Russell, 1940–
    The new world.
    (Illinois short fiction)
    I. Title.
PZ4.B2175Be [PS3552.A49]   813'.5'4   78-10646
ISBN 0-252-00722-0

for C. S.

"Iron sharpeneth iron;
so a man sharpeneth
the countenance of his friend."

Contents

Part I: Renunciation

"I will take this one window
with its sooty maps and scratches
so that my dreams will remember
one another and so that my eyes will not
become blinded by the new world."

—James Tate, "Fuck the Astronauts"

The Custodian

Rubin was forty-three years old when at last his father died and he was free. Free to marry, free to move to a new village if he wished, free to drink and smoke and sing bawdy songs. He was free to drive fast in an automobile and quit his job at the piano factory. He could buy flashy clothes and dirty books if he wanted, could eat Mexican food, go deer-hunting in the fall with the other men, and grow eggplants in his garden. He was free to enjoy modern art and foreign movies. He could read out-of-town liberal newspapers when he wanted, could go out without rubbers when it rained, could shout at the moderator at the town meetings, could play cards for money, could sell his old shaky car and buy a Japanese fastback coupe.

But he also knew that he was free *not* to do any of these things. Not a one. Thus he was free to continue living just as he had while his father had been alive—which in fact is what he chose to do, although he did note to himself that he wouldn't mind being married. It wasn't that Rubin had ever been forbidden to do what his father would not have done; rather, it was that Rubin simply had always been a kind man, and, because he knew that it would have saddened or displeased his father if he had done any of these things, he had decided not to do them. Even to the point that, until his father died, he had never really bothered to ask himself whether or not he actually *wanted* to drive fast in an automobile, for example, or eat Mexican food. He was relieved, therefore, when, upon asking, he discovered that he was in fact quite happy holding himself under the speed limit and sticking to good old-fashioned New England or, occasionally, Irish food.

The business about being free to marry, however—once the year of deep grieving had passed and he was able to think of his future without moaning aloud his father's name, Dad, Dad, Dad—that worried him. For, sometimes at night, lying alone in his narrow bed in the big house that he and his father had lived in together for the last twenty-seven years, ever since Rubin's mother had died, he would find himself tweaking his bristly moustache in paroxysms of lust, enduring glossy fantasies of buttocks and breasts, sweat and saliva, and he would be forced out of bed to pace through the entire house, flicking lights on and off as he entered and left the many rooms, staring in each room at the pictures on the wall, stern portraits painted in dim colors against dark backgrounds, all his ancestors, or studying the many faded photographs of his mother and father in ornate oval frames, reminding himself of the kind of man he was supposed to be, now that both his parents were dead.

His last name, in New England, was an old and honored one, as was his mother's maiden name, and all his male ancestors had been scholars, ministers, librarians—custodial people of various kinds— and as long as Rubin's father had been alive, Rubin, too, had participated in that tradition. Though he worked as a piano tuner in a piano factory, nevertheless, insofar as he had custody of his father, who, in turn, had custody of the naval history of the Jews, Rubin had been a custodian, too. But now, with his father gone, Rubin had nothing and no one in his custody, which is why he tended to think favorably about the idea of marriage, which, naturally, is what gave rise to the fantasies that made him wonder what sort of monstrous aberration he was.

He felt trapped. His lustful fits would lead him to study the faces of his ancestors, which would remind him of who he was supposed to be, who genetically and culturally he might expect himself to be, and this observation would lead him to the idea of marriage, and the idea of marriage would lead him implacably to the idea of women, the idea of slender necks and wisps of hair, of precise forearms and graceful calves, of thighs and plum-shaped breasts with coffee-colored nipples, of pelvic humps, sweating thrusts in half-light, mouths around genitals and genitals against genitals, and so on.

One night, caught twice in his circle, he experienced such frustration that he cursed his parents for having waited until they were in their fifties before having a child, cursed them for being so old that they themselves had become the objects of his custodial mission, rather than providing him with something like the naval history of the Jews, which would not die until he himself had died.

That was the night he decided to find a wife. The shame of finding himself cursing his beloved parents was simply too much to bear, and he knew that, unless he found a wife, he was bound to repeat himself. Reasoning carefully, as was his habit, he concluded that he would have good luck in seeking a wife if he started with women who were already married, women who in fact *were* wives, and since he had many men friends who happened to be married to wives, he began to visit these friends, to find out if one of their wives preferred him for a husband. If it turned out that there were several or many of them who preferred him, all the better, because then he would be free to choose, although, when he sat down on his mother's bed and thought about it, he liked all his friends' wives equally and would have great difficulty choosing among them.

Nevertheless, he began his search with energy and optimism, both of which were quickly rewarded, for he discovered among his friends' wives a dissatisfaction, once he had made his offer, that he had never imagined to exist, a discontent with their lives, their husbands, their children, their homes, which, when he described himself, his idea of what a husband was supposed to be and do, and his home, drew these women to him like paupers to a diamond find.

He was tactful enough not to present his case to the woman until the husband was either out of the room or otherwise distracted. Then he would slowly explain that he was looking for a woman to be his wife, now that his father had died, and he wondered how the idea appealed to her, the woman before him, in particular. He explained that he had never had a wife, as was already well known, but by that he meant that he had never actually slept with a woman, had never had a sexual relation with one, but he was certainly eager to begin such a relation.

Something about his voice, high, tight, restrained as if by iron clamps, and his manner of speaking, slow, careful without being hesitant, unembarrassed, dry, and also his language, which approximated that of a notarized statement verifying potency, must have seduced these women, must have touched an erotic fantasy or a deep and practically unconscious obsession that had never before been touched, because in every case he was answered with an immediate and passionate declaration of love and desire.

There was Deirdre, the wife of the carpenter, Ben, who, when Rubin made his query, had placed her hand onto his thigh, and, staring intently into his bright blue eyes, had asked when, now, tonight? He said no, that he first had to make a number of additional queries, but that he would let her know as soon as he had made a decision.

And there was Mame, the glamorous and rich wife of Roland, the real estate man, who had swiftly countered Rubin's offer with offers of her own—winters at Mallorca, summers in Casco Bay, rings, roadsters, and shad roe from Peru.

And there was Molly, wife of Boris the sculptor, whose panting response had included games with snakes he didn't even know the names of. Molly was from Mississippi, had tousled red hair cut short, athletic arms, and a soft mouth, and Rubin found the remark about the snakes somewhat intriguing.

Increasingly, as Rubin made the rounds of his friends' and neighbors' homes, eating dinner with them and afterwards discreetly proposing marriage to their wives, he was astonished by the alacrity of the wives' responses, their apparent urgency to become his wife. It did not, of course, occur to him that, in some crucial way, he was the perfect husband, for he was the son who was willing to be the father, the custodial waif, a lodestone which, when touched, converted unconscious or barely conscious needs and desires into precious possibilities. There was doubtless somewhere a female equivalent who was capable of releasing the barely acknowledged, corresponding fantasies of the husbands, but that was another story altogether, and no one, least of all the husbands in question, had imagined her yet.

Meanwhile, Rubin went about the town wreaking havoc among the marriages of his friends, for, as soon as he had left a house, the wife would turn into a creature that was unrecognizable to the husband. Deirdre, when she and her husband were alone, grabbed Ben by his brawny bicep and yanked him down on her, moaning, as he entered her warm body's welcoming gate, voluptuous obscenities and shrill cries of stark joy. Ben, not knowing what else to do, did what was expected of him, and found that while it gave him unexpected pleasure, it also filled his mind with the faces, bodies, and names of women he had often desired but had never dared seek, which in turn filled him with guilt and anger, first at himself, then at the objects of his desire, and finally at his wife, Deirdre, for reminding him of those women and his desire for them. And thus, for the remainder of the night and on into the days that followed, the couple fought bitterly, making the children cry and causing the neighbors to shake their heads in disgust.

Mame, when Rubin had left their home, had reacted similarly, and, yanking off her clothes, had draped herself in nothing but jewelry, necklaces, jade pendants that swung lewdly below her navel, bracelets on her ankles and upper arms, silver combs in her hair, rings on her toes, and she had danced for her startled husband a sensual, slow, undulating dance that made her jewelry glitter in the firelight, made the curve of her belly swell and swim across the room like a milk-colored moon, caused her large breasts to swing like the hindquarters of a loping female lion, until her husband, who was still seated on the sofa, open mouthed with astonishment and peculiar delight, ejaculated unexpectedly, which made him, a proud, controlled man, curse her, and in seconds they, too, were fighting bitterly, accusing each other of mad self-betrayals, hurling vases, paintings, wine glasses, bookends against the floor in rage.

And for Molly and her husband, Boris, it was the same. As soon as Rubin had left, Molly, murmuring the names of snakes Boris had never heard of, began to strip off her clothing, and, lapsing into a New Orleans accent, slightly French, she had draped her mouth across her husband's mouth, had run her red tongue down his throat, was flicking away the buttons of his shirt, nipping at the hairs of his chest and belly with her perfect small white teeth, grabbing the zipper of his pants between her teeth and, ripping it downward, ejecting his member into her open and wet mouth, which was always something she had refused to permit, in spite of his annual urgings. Amazed and gratified, he closed his eyes while Molly began to run her tongue along the dorsal vein of his erect and throbbing member, when suddenly, remembering the hysterical tenor of her past objections, he decided that he was being cruel and slightly perverse, and he felt his erection shrivel inside her mouth, shrinking in seconds from a leaping salmon to a merely nosey herring. Gulping air, he withdrew and zipped himself back up, buttoned his shirt, and prepared himself for the tongue-lashing that he knew would follow.

From here until the end, the story is predictable. Rubin, of course, would visit each of the three couples a second time, and this time he would see three suffering women, three women in great pain, with grey, pinched faces, tight mouths speaking hard, bitter language, three women catching their breaths at inappropriate moments, clattering the dishes against the sink or table, dropping the silverware, three women barking harshly at their children upstairs, ignoring their husbands, and feigning deep interest in Rubin's slow, deliberate speech. It would be awful for him. It would send him back into the night of his solitude, grieving for his father, groaning his name, Dad, Dad, Dad.

The Perfect Couple

In our town many years ago we agreed on most things, but there was never such clear unanimity as there was then concerning the inevitable marriage and lifelong happiness of Sally and Glenn. We believed in them. It should have been perfect (we still agree on that), a perfect match, the perfect girl for the perfect boy and the perfect boy for the perfect girl—the perfect couple. That's how we referred to them. "The perfect couple." Everyone in town knew it, we had all known it from the beginning, practically from before the two were even born, and we all said it, too, had said it from the beginning. We'd call each other up and, relaxed, confident, almost with relief, we'd say, "That Sally and that boy Glenn? I saw them coming out of the schoolhouse this morning, and don't you know, they're just perfect together!"

We never spoke with such frank confidence of the weather or of the crops or of our health. If things were going well, we were somberly grateful and thanked the Lord. If they were going badly, we cursed our luck and, without much hope, prayed for a change. Doubtless outsiders thought we were pessimistic, the way we stubbornly refused to take good fortune for granted and the readiness with which we accepted our own helplessness. But we thought of our attitude as nothing worse than a realistic timidity. To us it was a philosophy and it was rooted in our ancestors' experience and confirmed daily by our own. If a homely farmer married a pretty woman, we shrugged our shoulders and helplessly waited for her to betray him. If a child proved unusually clever, we waited with resignation for him to grow up and swindle his neighbors. If we had a mild winter, we knew that a crippling one would follow, and a meager crop always chased a bumper.

On the other hand, even though we found this timidity a necessity, as if it were an essential consequence of our philosophy, I think we were somehow secretly ashamed of it. It proved our pathetic helplessness in the face of history, nature, and the Lord. The idea of will, whether collective or individual, was nothing more than a conceit to us, nothing more than a stage setting for our most private fantasies. Giving that up was easy. But even so, we weren't sufficiently proud of what remained, our timidity, to call it humility.

That's why, looking back, I think it was, for us, a kind of original pride that we took in the clear inevitability of a marriage between those two children. If, for instance, you stepped into Cod's General Store for a few essentials, for salt and string, say, and Reverend Pease came in for his regular afternoon snack, you'd hear Cod say to the parson, "Wal, there's at least *one* wedding you can count on performing, eh, Reverend?" bringing it off with a public wink and friendly elbow jab, teasing the parson as if he were a fellow merchant and weddings were his merchandise.

The Reverend Pease always seemed to take this particular tease good humoredly (not the case with other teasings), and, sinking a considerable amount of literal comfort into his voice, as if weddings in fact were his merchandise and he had been assured of at least one sale, he'd nod his head in agreement and say, "Yes, indeed, yes, indeed," proudly.

For he wasn't much different from the rest of us. He too enjoyed being able, whenever possible, to count on things. He was a man of faith, of course, and years ago had bent his will to the Lord's with a decision which he called "momentous," but even so, even for such a man, it was still a pleasure and a bit of a relief when he could once in a while avoid crediting life's eventualities to the Lord's will, as if the Lord were not always the only One not surprised by the way things turned out. So, like everyone else in town during those years, the parson took pleasure and relief from the obvious perfection of the match. "It's nice," he would say, munching his cupcake, "to see a boy and a girl who seem to have been made for no one else on earth but each other."

Cod would look across his oilcloth-covered counter and smile seductively, as if the Reverend were slipping into secular platitudes and joining "the rest of mankind," as Cod defined his neighbors and himself. The Reverend, brushing crumbs from his red lips and round belly, would try to elevate the conversation. "It seems almost to have been preordained, doesn't it, Mr. Cod?"

And who could not agree with that? Certainly not Mr. Cod, and certainly not me, nor would you, if you could have seen the two, Sally and Glenn, and if you had known as much about their separate and shared pasts and the separate and shared past lives of their fathers as we thought we knew. You would've had to have possessed God's own universal eye not to have agreed with the Reverend. Or you would've had to have been able to read the future as easily and confidently as I and the others in town thought we could read the past.

Though most people believe the design of a future is implied by the design of a past, we, as I mentioned, did not. In this one case, however, we were convinced that the perfect symmetries that described Sally's and Glenn's lives and the lives of their fathers implied a perfectly symmetrical future. That was why we who possessed that lore felt relieved by our knowledge. It gave us the hope, perhaps foolish, that the future could be plotted, even if only this one time. After all, we were mostly poor people, hard-working, unsophisticated people, and therefore we were extremely conservative, especially when it came to first principles. For us, conservatism was the only reasonable alternative to superstition. And though I'm not like them in all ways (or I wouldn't be telling this tale in the first place), nevertheless I can't pretend that I don't respect their position, then and now, and share with them their longings for order, symmetry, and predictability. There is so much to be frightened of—pestilence, drought, disease, cosmic disorders of all kinds—that we must treasure those few lives whose descriptions give us a moment when we are not afraid.

It all goes back to the fathers, Saul and Gavin. Their story came out gradually, piecemeal, for they had been born and raised in a town similar to ours, but far off, and no one knew them until after they had come to live in our town, which was when they were already grown men, veterans of the war. It was Bulkley or Beau Key, or a place that sounded like that, where the two had been born and raised, and when they reached manhood, because it was wartime, they both enlisted and were sent to foreign lands, where they spent four years in trenches, apparently without performing acts of either heroism or cowardice. From what we later gathered, the two had been singularly close friends from earliest childhood. It was even thought that their parents might have been business partners.

None of this would be particularly notable if the two men, from the day they first appeared in our town, had not seemed, each of them, to complete the other. What one man lacked, the other possessed. Saul was the tall, thin one, Gavin the short, portly one. Saul was fair and hawk faced, Gavin was dark and moon faced. Saul was somber, soft spoken, measured, and in all ways restrained. Gavin was gay, brash, elaborate, and in all ways unrestrained. If Saul came into Cod's store, it was to purchase something he had determined a need for weeks before. If Gavin appeared, it was to chat, to see what was new on the shelves, to buy impulsively half a dozen different kinds of pickles that he would try out later on or perhaps not at all. If Saul was sometimes regarded as curt and unfriendly, Gavin was as often regarded as effusive and overfamiliar. If Saul was thought unduly cautious, Gavin was thought foolishly careless. And where one man was regarded as being neither one thing nor the other, so, too, was the other thought of as neither one thing nor the other. In that way, both men were thought to be not particularly generous, not particularly cruel, not particularly intelligent, and so on.

These symmetries no one noticed or, if he noticed, paid particular attention to, until after Saul and Gavin each had bought a farm on the same road, on the same side of the road, separated only by a single narrow strip of bottomland. They both made their purchases the same day, from the same agent, and tried, each of them separately, to buy the rich strip of bottomland that lay between the two farms. They failed, as we later learned, because the land was owned by a man named Oakes, a singer who had inherited it from his uncle, a man who once had been the town barber. Oakes, the singer, was itinerant and unsuccessful, at least insofar as he was not widely known and could not be contacted, even for the purpose of buying the unused strip of land he owned. In fact, very few of us remembered Oakes at all, and that he was known to be a singer depended solely on the tattered memories of the two high school teachers who remembered having taught the Oakes boy art and social studies. Although he had been adept at neither, both old women recalled his marvelous ability as a singer.

At first, none of us paid lengthy attention to this business of the land owned by Oakes or the question of his whereabouts. It was well known that first Saul, and then a few months later Gavin, too, tried carefully to get in touch with Oakes. The town clerk had given them the twelve return addresses Oakes had used when he'd paid his annual taxes on the land, but all the two men got for their troubles was *Return to Sender—Addressee Unknown*. To us, then, Saul's and Gavin's attempts to buy the land that linked their farms and their failure to do so were of no more than passing interest.

What finally fixed our wondering interest, however, was when, after their first harvest, the two men locked up their farms and left town for a period of what we later calculated to be thirty days, give or take a day, and returned, each of them carrying a child that was approximately two years old. First Saul and then Gavin stepped down from the train to the platform, and both of them with tender care adjusted the hats on the children's heads to protect them against the sudden blast of fall air. Those of us who happened to be in the station that day looked on in shock and bewilderment. We waved hello, but didn't know what to say, so we said nothing.

We had assumed from the day they first came to town that the two men were bachelors, and though now, with their return, we could no longer be sure, still, for all we ever really learned afterwards, maybe they *were* bachelors. It was impossible to know for sure. Neither man wore a wedding ring, and both carefully avoided any mention of a wife. The most we ever learned about the mothers of those two children was that they were both "deceased," and that we learned only when Saul and Gavin registered Sally and Glenn for school four years later. Of course we speculated and guessed about the women who had borne those two attractive and in many ways remarkable children. Cod, for example, was convinced that the mothers were foreign girls that Saul and Gavin had spent time with during the war. Sally and Glenn were supposed to be the results of that reckless time. "But that's the kind of man you just have to admire," Cod told us. "They played around and sowed their oats, sure, but now they're willing to pay the fiddler. That's one heck of a lot more than you can say for most young fellas today."

We agreed with Cod's latter observation, but most of us had difficulty accepting the former, his notion that the mothers were exotically foreign and that these children, who were now so carefully protected and nurtured with such domestic fastidiousness, were the offspring of some wild week in a sin-filled capital city in the middle of a foreign war. Not that it wasn't possible—we knew so little about Saul and Gavin that almost anything was possible. It just seemed too romantic to us, too brightly colored with optimism, and too structured by a justice that was kind to everyone involved. We were not a romantic people and we surely were not optimistic, and what sense of justice we had was deeply intertwined with our sense of punishment and cosmic revenge. This was surely not that.

So after a while, with all of us carping against him, Cod gave up his story and started promoting another, in which both mothers had been Saul's and Gavin's childhood sweethearts, recently married, and had died in childbirth, and the two infants had been left back in Belle Cay or Beau Key, or wherever, with aunts or grandparents, until the fathers could make homes that could accommodate them. This story we accepted as realistic, even probable, but for some reason no one seemed willing actually to believe it.

We saw very little of Sally and Glenn while they were growing up. Their fathers were strict and, as I mentioned, protective. But some things were known to us. Their physical attractiveness, for instance. On those occasions when they accompanied their fathers into town and we had a chance to view them shyly twining around their daddies' legs at the store, we were, to a man, impressed with the moderate grace and pleasant good looks possessed by both children.

And from the first, we were aware of certain symmetries about the children, for Sally resembled not her father, but Glenn's, and Glenn resembled not his, but Sally's. It was peculiar, and no one could see all four of them together without remarking on it. Once, after a visit by the four to a church bake sale, Reverend Pease, with a bit of amused wonder in his voice, was heard to say, "Kind of makes you think of that old story about the mix-up at the hospital, doesn't it?" Then he laughed, as if to dismiss the notion.

But it was enough to make you wonder—Sally's round, dark face and Glenn's long, blade-shaped, fair one, and Sally's ebullience, her noisy, high-spirited movements, and Glenn's somberness, his calm, restrained way of moving. So if you weren't of a mind to wonder about such things as the possibility of a mix-up at the hospital, you at least had to remark upon the symmetries. It was almost abstract, the way those two children were paired. If somebody noticed that one of them was right handed, sure enough, the next time they were in town it would become obvious to us all that the other child was left handed. If Cod offered the children two pieces of penny candy, one licorice and one mint, it always turned out that Sally conveniently loved licorice and Glenn preferred mint. And, just as with their fathers, if something was not particularly true of one child, it was not particularly true of the other, either, and in that way they both were not particularly well behaved, but not particularly mischievous, not particularly bright, but not noticeably slow, either, not what you'd call gorgeous, but not, in any way you could mention to a stranger, homely.

All such observations we were able to make within months of the children's surprising arrival in town, and as they grew up we discovered only additional symmetries and were never once forced to withdraw or deny a previously observed one. It was very early in their lives, then, before they had even gotten to school, in fact, that we began to think of Sally and Glenn as the perfect couple. And as they grew, we in town gradually found ourselves acting as a kind of cheering section for them, as if with our enthusiasm for their manifest symmetries we could encourage still more correspondences to appear and in that way could affect their shared connubial destiny.

We didn't know any of this at the time, of course. One rarely knows, at the time of his action, what values and assumptions he's acting on. It's only afterwards, when one's action has been organized by time and has been made to look ridiculous or heroic, that he can analyze and expose the principles that prompted him to behave so ridiculously or heroically in the first place. And if the man himself can't know at the time why he's behaving in a particular way, his neighbors surely can't know. For instance, it's probably true, when Saul and Gavin had first bought their farms and had each separately gone after the piece of land that lay between their respective properties, that both men could have offered an explanation for their actions. But I know it's equally true that we in town, even if we had known that explanation, probably would not have accepted it and would instead have drawn our own conclusions, saying things like, "They're both trying to make sure they have a neighbor they trust, and since they don't know who this Oakes fellow is, they must feel that if one or the other owns the land, they both can relax and rest assured that they won't have any boundary squabbles." Or we might have opined, "One of them must want the advantage over the other, and since both farms are of equal size, that strip between them will tip the balance." Or any number of things. One is never at a loss for an explanation for someone else's behavior, so long as one's not overly concerned with being correct, and, after all, neighbors rarely care about being correct. What terrifies a people is the chance that they might not be able to come up with an explanation at all, that Cod, for one, might some day have to say, "Boys, I don't know *why* they want that little piece of land," and no one will be able to answer Cod's not knowing with a quick explanation to which the rest of us can shake our heads sagely up and down, expressing in that roundabout way the means by which we ourselves happen to be in this mysterious world, as if all along, in giving our definitions of others, our intent were merely to define ourselves to ourselves.

Take that Oakes' land, now. We did settle, finally, on an explanation for their having sought to buy it. The consensus was that Saul and Gavin were looking for a neighbor they could be sure wouldn't ever give them boundary trouble. To us, that seemed a sensible thing to be looking for, and for a few years we all rested comfortably with that explanation, until someone, I'm not sure who, noticed that every spring, when Saul and Gavin each plowed the field on his farm that adjoined the Oake's land, he cut a new furrow from it, so that every year Oakes' uncultivated land was narrowed by two furrows. Another way to look at it would be to notice that every spring both Saul and Gavin picked up an extra strip of rich bottomland. We looked at it both ways. Even so, the trouble with these particular observations (and we all had to go out there on some excuse or other to confirm them) was that they made us question our prior explanation for Saul's and Gavin's initial interest in the land. It was no longer all that clear to us that their interest was not simply one of greed, that it was merely, as we had thought, "sensible."

And of course neither Saul nor Gavin did anything to deny such an impression. Quite the contrary. With each passing year they gained another slab from either side of Oakes' land for their own use. For who was to stop them? Oakes kept paying his taxes, mailing in his money from places like Biloxi and Greenville and conveniently never appearing in person. And as a result, every year the land he was paying taxes on got narrower and narrower, until, naturally, because it was not, after all, an especially wide strip of land in the first place, the two old friends' farms were growing to be at last adjacent.

We had watched this process for years, just as for years we had watched Sally and Glenn and, with delight and something not unlike pride, had seen them approaching adulthood and imminent marriage with one another. In a small town things don't change so much as their true natures get revealed. And it wasn't until Sally and Glenn were almost grown, and Oakes' land had almost disappeared into the farms owned by Saul and Gavin, that we finally realized that there was a connection between the two. Though, obviously, it wasn't a cause-and-effect connection, nonetheless we knew that there was more to it than a mere chronological concurrence, a coincidence. So about that time we started behaving as if we believed that one event was impossible without the other, that if Saul and

Gavin did not finally join their separate pieces of land by appro-
priating, row by row, Oakes' land, then the offspring could not
marry. And because we were behaving as if we believed this, it
gradually became clear to most of us that in fact we *did* believe it.
That's how strong the connection was.

So when the spring that the fields would be joined at last came
around, on the day that we knew Saul and Gavin would finish their
plowing, a large number of us drove and walked out there, many of
us dressed in our fine clothes, as if we were going to a wedding. We
gathered in a quiet group behind Sally and Glenn, who, having
taken up positions at the end of the final, unplowed row, were
holding hands, facing their fathers' oncoming plows, smiling
nervously into each other's faces and bravely rehearsing the speech
they had prepared.

Slowly the brown, boney heads of the mules pulling the plows
approached them, the two men side by side driving the animals on,
each plow curling a thick lip of black earth onto the shoulder of the
adjacent furrow, and when the mules arrived face to face with the
unyielding, hand-holding boy and girl and the crowd of spectators
behind them, the animals turned aside, one in the direction of Saul's
farm, the other in the direction of Gavin's, as if headed for their
respective barns. The boy, Glenn, was standing on the side of the
land that was towards Saul's farm, and Sally was on Gavin's side,
each of the sweethearts placed so as to face the other's parent, so
that, when the mules turned and the two exultant plowmen, Saul
somber and Gavin grinning, had come along behind and hollered,
"Whoa!" each man had found himself unexpectedly facing the
other's child.

Glenn spoke first. He announced to Sally's father, Saul, in a
clear, sober voice his love for the girl and his desire to marry her,
and then Sally told Glenn's father, Gavin, the same thing. There
was a moment's silence, while the mules steamed in the hot afternoon
sun and the freshly turned earth settled moistly beneath its own
weight. We in the crowd shifted our feet nervously but without
apprehension. A pair of crows in a larch gawked, and a lone cloud
scudded towards the horizon.

The moment passed. Saul clucked to his mule, Gavin to his, and the two old men lifted their plowshares clear of the soil and headed for their barns. As he drove away, Saul turned around slightly and snarled over his shoulder at Glenn, ordering him off his land, and at the same instant Gavin snarled and ordered Sally off his. Then the two glared at us, once, and drove intently on.

Silently, without a moment's hesitation, as if we all had pressing business elsewhere, we left. But the two grown children refused to move, except to turn and face each other and hold each other's hands. We all went swiftly back to town, to our shops and houses, shocked and feeling suddenly, unexpectedly, humiliated, but unable to say to ourselves or to anyone else how and why.

Well, obviously, this is not the end of the story. We were fortunate, perhaps, in that we were able to learn later what happened back at the farms after we had left. Apparently, Sally and Glenn had ignored their fathers' orders to remove themselves from the land of the other, and the couple had continued standing there as before, holding hands, looking into one another's eyes, surely shocked, dejected, despairing. Their future must have suddenly looked to them like a fancy, a whim, an idle, hopeless dream.

At dusk, Saul and Gavin, independently of each other, or so it seemed, returned to the field to see why their children were not at home, and they saw the two still standing where they had stood before, Glenn in the furrow Saul had plowed and Sally in the one Gavin had plowed. Furious, each father had commenced to yank and beat at his child, while the children yanked and fought back, refusing to be separated or moved.

Desperately they fought to hold onto their spot, and the fathers fought just as desperately to root them out of it, to yank them free of its force, the four in sharp, dark profile against the silvery sky, pulling back and forth, thrashing, slapping, grabbing at one another in silence. When, suddenly, they were stopped in mid-motion and frozen there into a tableau by the sound of a man's singing. It was the voice of the singer, Oakes, high, clear, wildly sad in the twilight, the voice of a man who, wandering through the region, had decided to come back to his hometown for a look at the place he had left and the land he had inherited from his uncle. He sang, in a sweet tenor that wasn't all that bad, this song:

> I've traveled all this high wide land
> Seeking fortune and some fame,
> I've climbed the peaks and walked the sand
> With hopes to carve my name
> Behind me in the hearts and minds
> Of the lonely and the sad,
> So if you've not yet heard my name,
> You've reason to be glad,
> Oh, you've reason to be glad.

When the singer had drawn close enough to the four dark combatants to see them, he asked them what they were doing there in his "little old piece of this good earth," which was how he put it. Breathless, Sally and Glenn, sensing in the singer the presence of an ally, explained why they were struggling. Indeed, he was an ally, and, proving his allegience, he forthwith offered them the land upon which they were fighting. It was to be a wedding present, he told them, and at this point Saul suddenly grabbed at his own forehead, that high, narrow brow, with his huge hands and at once fell groaning painfully to the ground, and mere seconds later Gavin started babbling incoherently and walking in tiny circles. Horrified, for Sally and Glenn realized that one father had suffered a stroke and the other had gone mad, the couple fled, down the road towards town, leaving the singer seated on a boulder beside the road, humming to himself and now and then letting a line or two escape his smiling lips.

From here, I suppose you might say the story got sadder and sadder for Sally and Glenn. We in town don't happen to feel that way, but we can understand how an outsider might. When the couple arrived in town and word of what had happened to their fathers got back to us, they found us not quite as supportive of their venture as we had been in the past. The circumstances had changed, and it was difficult for us not to condemn the couple for betraying their daddies and causing the two hard-working old men such grief, pain, and madness. "It does no one any good if you push coincidence too far," the Parson explained to them. Cod agreed wholeheartedly, as did practically everyone else in town. After all, we had principles and couldn't ignore them.

So the couple moved on. We heard later that they had many adventures together, that they had drifted downriver for a time from village to town to city, and on out to town and village again, until, in despair, they had set out in a small rowboat to cross the river, and, halfway across, weeping, they had withdrawn a plug from the bottom of the boat. As it filled with water and sank, they could be heard from a distance singing to each other the only line from the singer's song that apparently they could remember. Over and over they sang, until at last they went under, "You've reason to be glad, oh, you've reason to be glad."

That's probably apocryphal, or at least exaggerated. People tend to tell stories that reveal the way they feel about the world, not the way the world feels about them. So you've got to be careful. If you're going to believe a story, you ought to know exactly what the story is supposed to be about, which means that you ought to know something about the person telling it. We, incidentally, got the story of what happened at Saul's and Gavin's, that day following our departure for town, from the singer, Oakes, of all people. Eventually, he had followed Sally and Glenn into town, and it seemed he enjoyed the town, or else was tired of wandering, because he opened up a barber shop and tried taking up where his uncle had left off. Unfortunately, the town was no longer able to support a barber as well as it had in his uncle's day, probably because everyone did his own shaving now, and Oakes, after a few years, went out of business and closed up the shop. He left town, and we have never heard from him again, except once a year, when he sends in his tax money for that strip of land out there between Saul's and Gavin's.

Saul and Gavin? They live in town now, spend most of their time quietly together on the porch of Cod's store, keeping track of things in the town and roundabout the area. Saul has to be careful of his heart, and Gavin can't get too excited. They're almost like an old husband and wife, the way they're always together and the way they seem to know what the other is thinking. It's a comforting thing to see. Neither of them ever speaks of his child, and because we would never be so cruel as to bring up their names, it's almost as if the children had never even been born. Especially now with Oakes gone.

A Sentimental Education

How could she have been such a fool? Veronica wondered, while the man named Vic, a billy goat of an auto mechanic, banged against her from behind. They were down in the cool darkness of the grease pit in the garage where Vic worked, in the shadow of the grease- and mud-clotted underside of a Chevrolet Nomad that Vic was supposed to be lubricating, and would have been, if it hadn't been for Veronica's presence there in the grease pit.

She hadn't especially wanted to lie on her back in the slime among the tools and oily rags, so Vic had suggested that she position herself on her hands and knees, which had worked out rather well—she knew she wouldn't have much trouble washing off her hands and knees—but she hadn't expected the sudden spurt of self-consciousness she was at the moment experiencing and which was responsible for her proceeding to question how she could have been such a fool, she, Veronica Stetson, the only and pampered child of big-in-oil Earl Stetson, she who was a product of boarding schools in the South and the finest finishing school in the East, was fluent in five languages, all of them foreign, was a concert-level pianist and an Olympic-quality freestyle swimmer, was blonde and blue eyed, long and tanned of limb, high cheekboned, nose like a tiny isosceles triangle, mouth that suggested gaiety, intelligence and sensuality all at once, teeth shaped for nips and nibbles or biting at the bubbles of champagne—and yet here she was, mucking about in a muumuu in a grease pit with a grease monkey at ten o'clock on a Sunday morning.

It didn't make sense. What was happening to her? she queried. Was she mad? This was beyond slumming, she observed, remembering a wild weekend in Brownsville. Had she lost all sense of proportion? Were all her connections—to her true self and where and what she came from—broken, sundered, lost?

And why now, why so suddenly, was she asking these questions? Why hadn't they come up earlier, when they would have been just as appropriate as now? At nine o'clock in the morning, for instance, an hour ago, when she had been spread-eagled in the back of Vic's buzzard-black pickup truck. She remembered Vic's face above hers, sweating, unshaven, unworried, dreamily drifting along in time to his own smooth and even strokes. She remembered thinking then that whatever was happening to her, it was extremely interesting. Was exactly what she had *hoped* would happen. Was *just fine. God,* she had thought, *this is just fine!*

But not now, not this time. This sure was *not* just fine. This was awful. Crazy, maybe. If anyone she knew could see her at this instant, he would say, "Ronnie Stetson's *really* flipped out this time. I mean, *really,* with a grease monkey named *Vic?* In a *grease* pit? At ten in the *morning?* For the *second* time? *Ugh.*"

So why the sudden change? she asked herself. What's the difference between the bed of a pickup truck at nine and a grease pit an hour later? It didn't bother me then. I didn't once think it was strange, let alone question my sanity. That's what actually makes me question my sanity *now,* she observed, the fact that I *didn't* question it earlier. Or even before that, last night, say, when everything started getting out of control.

What had happened last night was that, after dinner, she had kissed Mummy and Daddy goodbye while they were still at table, and then, wishing them bon voyage, for they were packed and dressed for an evening flight to Mexico City, she'd feigned headache and fatigue and had dashed up the curving staircase to her yellow silk bedroom, where she had stripped off her satin clothes and had disguised herself in the green corduroy muumuu and blue-starred tennis shoes.

She had long before this decided to call herself Martha, a name that to her was the opposite of Veronica. She had decided to claim that she was a recently divorced young woman who'd left her baby at home watching TV because if she, Martha, didn't get the hell out of the house alone tonight she was going to flip right out. The kid was starting to drive her nuts. She wasn't some kind of rich lady who could pass the kid off to a nursemaid or something or could send the kid off to boarding school somewhere. No, she had to live with this kid, day in and day out, cooking for it, cleaning it, wiping its nose, and mending its clothes. If she didn't get a break, she was going to go nuts. And she didn't care who knew it.

She slipped down the back stairs to the kitchen, went out the back door and took the gardener's orange Pontiac station wagon, and, racing downtown, then crosstown, along littered streets lined with pool parlors, pawnshops, and taverns, she finally stopped and parked the car in front of a randomly selected bar & grill with green, painted-over, plate glass windows. WINK'S BAR & GRILL.

That's where she met Vic—tall, hawkfaced, blackhaired, wearing tight Levis and a black T-shirt with the pocket over his heart stretched around a hardpack box of Parliaments. At first she saw him only from behind. He was leaning over the jukebox in the back, studying the song titles as if trying to memorize them, and as he tapped his foot in time to the music, his back muscles rippled rhythmically. Veronica had never seen back muscles ripple in quite that way. *Unconsciously, almost cruelly,* she thought. She loved the way they seemed to move in spite of themselves. She decided that the movement was essentially proletarian. She decided that it was a class characteristic that functioned simultaneously as an aid in manual labor, a sexual signal for purposes of selective breeding, and, like the so-called blues, a spiritually uplifting means of self-expression for the otherwise inarticulate. Naturally, she was touched.

And when Vic strolled back to the bar and sat upon the stool that was next to the one she had taken, she leaned over, wet her pink-painted lips and asked him for a light, then brazenly informed him that she had never seen back muscles quite like his before. Which was true enough. She hadn't. But it was the kind of thing Veronica Stetson would have said anyhow.

His eyes were the color of a mud hen, and they twinkled when he laughed and grabbed her shapely knee and said, "Hello there, girlie, whaddaya doin' out all alone tonight? Didn't your mama tell you never to talk to strangers?" he asked, grinning, and he chucked her under the chin with the thumb and forefinger of his right hand.

They talked, and when, a few minutes later, he asked her if she wanted to see his tattoo, she was thrilled and knew in her heart for the first time that in leaving home tonight she had made the right decision.

But it was not merely the hectic search for novelty that had driven her from the coldly glittering sanctity of her parents' home tonight. It was boredom. What she felt compelled to call *"colossal* boredom." "Ennui," she had said. "The consequence of being able to predict practically every word and act of every person I meet." It was as if neither she nor anyone she met or knew had alternatives, a condition she claimed to have endured for most of the last two years. Since graduation. She knew it couldn't go on indefinitely without eventually making her cynical. A French novel had told her that, and she had relayed it to her parents, her friends, and, tentatively, her psychiatrist. All of whom had assured her that in no way could she become more cynical than she already was. Indeed, her psychiatrist had felt that her cynicism was a defensive reaction designed to protect her against what she perceived as her essential vulnerability, which in turn was the result of what she perceived as a premature loss of innocence. A not unusual set of perceptions among members of her particular class, he had pointed out with a smile.

She, nonetheless, knew slightly better than they. For she alone knew truly what innocence yet remained, what romance was still available to her, what hope. And though they remained in clots only, not as freely flowing streams, she treasured them, innocence, romance, and hope, as if they were Christian virtues, and she had determined to preserve them, at least for her own use, if no one else's.

To preserve such virtues, however, she first had to locate and participate in them. She knew that much. This meant that she would have to expose herself to worlds either that hitherto she had denied herself or that had been kept from her, as if across a moat, by her parents, her class, her wealth and education, her good looks and charm. No innocence there, she knew. No romance. No hope.

Thus, she had imagined Martha, a woman her own age who, in spite of a native intelligence, good looks, and child-like charm, attributes Martha possessed but simply was not aware of, and because of her class, her poverty and ignorance, could predict nothing, absolutely nothing, not even rain from a gathering of storm clouds. Martha was a woman who, therefore, in Veronica's mind, was totally innocent, uncontrollably romantic, and eternally hopeful.

And tonight, at WINK's, after months of obsessively conjuring the image, invoking another woman's dreary past and opaque future, reading the drabness of the woman's present as if it were a sacred text or entrails or dice cast to determine eventualities in another world, dreaming the bland life of a woman whose life had otherwise gone wholly ignored, unloved, utterly disregarded, Veronica had successfully transformed herself. It was working. Vic asked her what her name was, and she told him, and, as if by magic, he began calling her Martha. She also let it out that she was recently divorced. Her ex-husband had been a truck driver for a bread company, and her daughter, Pearl, four years old, was home watching TV. A sweet kid but she can really be a pain in the you-know-where sometimes. You gotta do everything for them at that age. Just thank God they're old enough to sit in front of a TV while Mama goes out for a few hours of relaxation.

Vic took all this in, believed it, made it real for her. That was about the time he had shown her the tattoo—an angel's head, crudely drawn on his right forearm, and, in a half-circle above the angel's blonde curls, the words, *Remember Death.*

Martha gasped. Veronica lurched forward in her seat and caught herself staring.

Gently Vic told her that his tattoo was all he ever needed to keep him from getting down. It was kind of like his religion, he explained. He used it to remember life, because whenever he thought of death, he told her, he immediately thought of life. "Simple!" he grinned.

Veronica thought that was the most original thing she had ever heard. The realism of the proletariat, she reflected, invoked as a philosophic position in its entirety by a simple mnemonic device which doubled, functionally, as body decoration. *Oh, the unconscious mind,* she purred to herself.

They danced the North Texas Push several times and went to a second bar & grill. Then a third and a fourth, where, around midnight, Vic casually suggested that she come out to his trailer for a nightcap.

She drove her station wagon, followed the red dots of Vic's Ford Ranchero out of town to a trailer park located near the thruway to the airport. It was the same trailer park that, from the air-conditioned back seat of her Daddy's limousine, she had noticed so many times with irritation and disdain. Because it was so *ugly*. She could hear herself telling Daddy, "They look like pink and blue railroad cars that've been scattered by a train wreck! It's hard to believe that people are even *willing* to live in those boxes, let alone that they *want* to! Well, there's your industrial revolution for you," she had added sadly. Daddy said he wasn't sure he could agree with that.

But now, tonight, as she slid out of her station wagon, she knew that after this she would look upon that pocket of lower-middle-class metal-and-plastic housing quite differently. Yes, sir. And that pleased her immensely, convinced her yet again that she, Veronica Stetson, was doing a *good,* a *wise,* an *enlarging* thing. She was preserving her innocence, and she was altering the world to make it safe for romance, and she was fixing things so that a hopeful person didn't always have to be a fool.

I'll have to write about this afterwards, she thought as she stepped up the cinder blocks to the door of the trailer, a small but sleek, pale green, French colonial model with a mansard roof.

She accepted one more drink of Canadian whiskey and 7-up and then proceeded to couple with Vic, both of them still at least partially dressed, first on the Formica-topped kitchen counter, then on the Danish modern coffee table, and at last, naked, in the enormous bed that, to her surprise and delight, Vic made from a couch simply by yanking a lever at the side. Vic's sexual straightforwardness and prowess and his wordless hunger, his simple greed, that too amazed and delighted her, and in the midst of making observations to herself about the need for the lower classes to express their emotional lives with their bodies, their tendency to physical overdevelopment, their need to define sexual roles strictly in terms of dominance, she found herself having sudden, unexpected orgasms, *Wham! Wham! Wham!* and she would catch the tail end of a cattle drive of obscenities drifting from her lips.

Finally Vic rolled off her and fell asleep, mouth open, snoring loudly, and she, Martha, alone in the darkness, began to wonder how she should feel about her child, Pearl, her little girl curled up in the tattered armchair and finally asleep in front of the buzzing white eye of the television screen.

Getting carefully out of bed, she tiptoed to the door. Just as she turned the handle to open it, she heard Vic's voice behind her, angrily demanding to know where she was going. "What gives?" he barked darkly.

She whimpered that she was worried about Pearl, and he told her to call her on the phone if she was worried, he didn't want any woman of his making it with him all night and then taking off before breakfast. "Hey, I think more of you than *that!*" he explained. The way he saw it, they had a real thing going together, not just some Saturday night bed-thumping kind of thing.

She returned slowly to his bed. If she phoned Pearl now, she'd only wake her up. Let the child sleep, she admonished herself, and, smiling in the cool moonlight that fell in wedges through the venetian blinds, she pulled the covers to her dimpled chin, and after a while, to the sound of Vic's peaceful snoring, fell asleep.

In the morning, she was up before him, scrambling eggs, and, while he dressed, she told a little fib (that's what she called it), said that she'd gotten up early to call Pearl and everything was fine at home because she'd gotten a babysitter for the day and now she wanted to spend the day with him, maybe at the beach?

He was glad to know that her daughter was all right. "Terrific the kid's okay," he said, stuffing eggs into his mouth. But no beach. He had to work today at the garage. But she could keep him company down there if she wanted, because it was Sunday and no one else had to work, and there wouldn't be much business anyhow.

How exciting, thought Martha. Just the two of them all day at the garage. He could tell her the names of tools. Maybe he could teach her how to pump gas.

He drove her with him to the garage in his Ranchero, and, while she was helping him remove a pair of new tires from the back, he came up behind her, and, placing his large hands onto her rump, pulled her down onto him, turned her over onto her back, and in seconds had her spread-eagled under him, a whitewall tire on either side of them as he stroked swiftly beneath the morning sun behind the garage.

Then, an hour later, in the grease pit, it had been the same—sudden, good humored, but urgent. And with no real alternative. The occasion was such that Vic would be expected by an audience of Vics to behave precisely as he was behaving. And for Martha to have behaved any differently from the way she was now behaving was unthinkable. And when she realized that, that absence of an alternative, for both of them, not just for him and not just for her, that's when she had wondered, *How could I have been such a fool?*

He was behind her, reaching around with his hands and clutching her breasts, and she could see his tattoo. She read the words again, *Remember Death,* but instead of remembering death, as instructed, and thinking of life, as Vic had done, she remembered life, first her old one and then her new one, and thought of death, and at that instant she felt Vic jerk and knew that his sperm had entered her and had impregnated her, and she knew that she would have a daughter, that she would name her daughter Pearl, and she promised herself that never, never, never would Pearl have to stay home alone all night watching TV while her mother was out drinking and laying with garage mechanics named Vic. And then Martha promised herself that even though Pearl would be rich, advantaged, educated, comforted, and though her life would be different from this, no grease pits, no ominous tattoos, no house trailers, no convertible sofas, it would nevertheless be a life with many alternatives at every moment. It would be a life of romance, of innocence, and of hope. That's what Veronica Stetson knew.

About the Late Zimma (Penny) Cate: Selections from Her Loving Husband's Memory Hoard

For forty-five years Penny and I lived together in holy wedlock—each of us, like most people, suffering from his and her own afflictions of the body and of the spirit. Unlike most people, however, Penny and I were each able to bandage over our afflictions with the other's strengths. We were not forced to "go it alone." My strength covered her weakness, and hers mine; for while my weakness was mostly of the human, spiritual type, hers was solely of the body—that crippled, frail body of hers, a vessel of relentless pain for close to forty years, excruciating pain she never complained of, wincing merely, then bravely smiling up from her wheelchair into my face or the face of one of the doctors or nurses who attended her so faithfully and competently, especially in these last two months and eight days during which she lay dying. She provided us all with the example and image of Jesus Christ Himself on His Cross, so that we might sharpen our dulled faith and come to know Him better and take comfort from that knowledge. In that way she made it possible for us to endure her end with the calm that approaches joy—her last and His greatest gift. And I know that's how she wanted me to understand her dying.

Last night, as I looked down at her while she lay in her final bed, the flowers, red and white chrysanthemums, carefully arranged behind her in a horseshoe by the thoughtful attendants of Waters Funeral Home, her mouth gently pressed into a sweet smile, her silver hair curled and combed with tender care by George Waters himself—she looked so natural to me, so naturally content, that when, with her cousins and a few of our neighbors, I knelt by the casket to pray, I recalled how she had looked to me that summer night forty-five years ago, when we made our decision to marry—in defiance of both our parents, who, because we were second cousins, had tried strenuously to separate us. But that night, while walking home from a band concert, we made up our minds and eloped to Albany, where, at the age of eighteen, we became man and wife. And though we were cousins, it was only after we had become man and wife that we really began to grow together. Before then we had been no more alike than any two members of the same species. But from that day forth we became as a single plant formed of two stems, and no gardener but the Highest could tell us apart. I mean spiritually, of course. I remember that closeness.

We were both healthy and strong then. I, in particular, was exceptionally strong and supple, and though only eighteen years old and the youngest member of my class, I was the best athlete. All muscle. I paid for my two years of Bible study at Gordon College and a year in Germany and another in Israel by wrestling and boxing, weight lifting, and acrobatics. I had a stunt-and-dance routine that I performed for churches and missions to hold the congregations' attention and to show them that, with Jesus in your heart, nothing is impossible. In that way, Penny and I traveled throughout the U.S., Old Mexico, Cuba, Canada (where I fought the middle-weight champion of Canada to a draw), Germany, where I studied the theologians, and the Holy Land itself, where I studied the very dirt Christ trod.

That reminds me of a little story about Penny that may illustrate what kind of a woman she was, for even though I was the athlete and had fought the Canadian champion to a draw, the real athlete and the real champ was my wife Penny.

After our wanderings in the desert, we finally settled in Crawford, New Hampshire, near where we had been raised, to make our peace with our families and our lives with each other. I decided to support us by chopping wood while I furthered my education in the serenity of the forests by taking correspondence courses. Studying to become a Master of Divinity, I became instead a master of ax and bucksaw; that fall I built both a two-room cabin at the foot of Blue Job Mountain and the basis for an informed faith in the One God.

When I think now of that year, 1928, I think of the spring day I finished chopping out four cords a day for four successive days. Sixteen cords of wood in less than a week! It was a mile up the hill from our cabin to the woodlot along a crooked snow path, snow falling day and night, me stripped to the waist from sunrise all day long, trees falling across each other like the timbers of a collapsing barn— and though the snow was a Godsend and helped me ease the logs downhill, the greatest aid in my Herculean labors was that tiny young woman with the curling blonde hair who trudged up the trail three times each day whistling like a bluebird in her blue-and-white snowsuit, a knapsack with coffee and chicken sandwiches in it on her back, our dog Tray leaping through the snow ahead of her. What great powers God has bestowed upon women! She practically electrified me with her visits and three times a day succeeded in turning me into a human chopping machine!

Then, on July 12, 1931—I'll never forget the date—the police chief of Crawford, a man now deceased (which is why I will not name him), falsely arrested me, and once again my wife Penny proved that her worth exceeded her name. I was "booked" because I happened to be taking a hurt man to the doctor so that he would not bleed to death. It doesn't matter now how he got hurt, except to insist again that of course it was an accident, and it doesn't matter now who the man was, except to explain again that much of my family, like most New England families, treated each other worse than strangers.

Anyhow, a state policeman and the chief drove out to Blue Job to question my wife, but what they saw there when they arrived was something they obviously did not expect to see—a neat log cabin squarely built, with an attractive, well-dressed woman in high heels standing in the doorway! That and the tall, wind-tossed pine trees and Tray basking in the sun on the pine needles that blanketed the ground must have shocked them, because when they found out from my wife Penny that I was an honest woodsman and a man studying to become a preacher, they panicked, yes sir, and, instructing my wife to have papers in court proving that I was what I, and then she, had said I was, they turned their car around and drove like crazy back to town to fix up a kangaroo court, leaving my wife to walk seven miles out of the woods alone.

The presence of that courageous, determined wife in the courtroom, her heels worn down from the tough walk, her angry face flushed and fearless, must have made the judge want to pull his cloak over his head. The verdict—he practically mumbled it— "Guilty. Fifty-five dollars fine, and chop it out of those woods in three days or go to jail!"

I looked down at my tiny Penny. "Should I appeal?"

Without a second's hesitation, she replied in a loud voice that everyone in the room could hear. "Call their bluff!" she cried.

The chief carried us home in his Ford at three P.M., and, after thanking him for the lift, I asked him to come back at the same time in three days and went right to work, chopping through the long night, with a buggy lantern hanging from a branch and, up above, the moon, almost full for three nights in a row. I could hear the battery radio playing hymns down below in the cabin, could glimpse the kerosene lamp in the window, both assuring me as I worked that "All is well!" And every three hours I would hear a whistling, and the dog Tray would come leaping up the trail ahead of my wife Penny as she brought me the coffee and chicken sandwiches.

In that way the three days of my harrowing passed quickly, and when the chief arrived at three P.M. sharp, he saw thirty-eight cords of wood neatly stacked, a dollar-fifty a cord, a fifty-five dollar payment for the fine, plus two dollars extra, which I told him was payment for the transportation he had provided us. I looked that man in the eye and said, "If you come to Blue Job, you'll find some hard-working people, and you'll find God there, too!"

Well, police rarely apologize. They just grin, and the chief just grinned. But he knew I had him. Thanks to Penny.

But all that happened to us back before her beautiful strong legs began to grow crooked, her knees and ankles deformed and weak, the joints brittle and dry, and we had to move into town. There, for the first twelve and a half years, she was able to work the cash register and tend the counter at the old Faucher Market on the Heights, giving service to all who approached her, even though they came from all walks of life. I was unable to find work in the town as a woodsman, so I stayed home and continued with my studies.

The little boys and girls, how well I remember them. They would ask for Penny to fill their ice-cream cones, and the extra scoop on top always let her slide swiftly into their hungry little hearts. Unable to bear children on her own, she gave all the more to the children of strangers. They believed in what she stood for, even without being able to name it, because she was an idol with a soul inside that cried out to them, "Let Jesus lead you!"

And if the proof and the truth thereof lie with the facts, He *did* lead them, because some of those little girls today are schoolteachers, nurses, secretaries in government offices, and wives of important men. And the little boys grew up, too, receiving A's in their classes, going on to become members of the police force, firemen, ministers, lawyers, doctors, all of them with vocations. Not a rotten apple in the barrel!

All those fine young men and women were sent by my wife Penny on a mission of success, their large hearts filled with the love of Jesus. Some are now the best lab technicians in the Concord Hospital, dental assistants, a former mayor's wife, a postmaster. A former governor and his wife sent my wife Penny a Christmas card every year for seventeen years, a beautiful card with a picture of their wonderful family, their animals, and their home, with impressive thoughts denoting that love and God in a home make it a castle, something that Penny and I always believed in, no matter how humble our abode, and tried to teach to others.

I remember the time our landlord, Mr. Dubey, made a mistake in the rent receipt, crediting us with two months' rent instead of one. I was coming home from the market and was about to cross the street with a pushcart full of groceries. It was one of those raw, cold days when the snow on the ground looks like bleached leather and the sky is like a wet sheet. Suddenly I saw Mr. Dubey stride out the door of our apartment house, and a second later I saw my wife Penny pop out the same door in her wheelchair, roll down the ramp I'd built her to the icy sidewalk and around the corner to where she finally caught him in his laundromat. She parked her chair right in front of him and would not move it until he had written out a new rent receipt and had torn up the old one. She could have waited a few minutes more for me to come home, and I would have gone after Mr. Dubey myself, but Penny never asked anyone else to do what she considered to be either her own or God's work, and she told me that correcting Mr. Dubey on the rent receipt was both.

I remember waking up the morning she died. The sun was up already, so I knew I had overslept. I went to the window and looked out at the slush-filled street. It was going to be a day of melting, I could tell, even though it was still early in the morning. Sometimes you just know things ahead of time, without knowing how or why you know them. But I never knew Penny would die.

When they told me she was dead, I started talking about our life together. It was at the hospital. They had called me on the telephone and had said, "You better get right over here, Mr. Cate," so I had rushed out the door and had taken a taxi all the way over, in spite of the three dollars it cost. When I walked into her room, she was gone. They had already changed her bed and had the room ready for the next patient. That's when I started talking, to the nurses, the attendants, the doctors, anyone who would listen.

Somehow, as long as I keep talking, it seems more like she hasn't died yet, if you know what I mean. I wonder how long this can last. But we were married for forty-five years, you know, so there's quite a lot of my life to remember before I run out of things to say. People must do this a lot. It's probably something given to us by God to help us get around the hard parts of life.

The Conversion

When Alvin Stock was sixteen years old, he once again found himself loathesome and, after a brief period of great longing and pain, underwent a religious conversion. This discovery, that he was loathesome, took place one Saturday morning early in March, when, while sitting dejectedly on the edge of his rumpled bed, he concluded that he was slime, a bug, an animal lower than carrion-eaters. He was a soulless bag of appetites, a disease, a corruption of lusts. He was an absence of will.

Though it was not unusual for Alvin, upon waking, to see before him his very own erect penis, and then to observe promptly that he was slime, a bug, jackal, etc., it was also not unusual, after he had urinated, washed, and dressed himself, for him to be able to forgive himself by means of the simple strategy of not giving himself another thought, so that by the time he arrived in the kitchen for breakfast, he was likely to be allowing to himself that he was the prince of this land, something of a genius, and also a potentially great athlete. He saw himself as a young man of gifts, a youth whose promise was matched only by the abundance of his ambition, and his purity.

But this time it was different. After he had urinated, washed, and dressed himself, he had walked, on this new day, back from the bathroom to his bedroom and had sat down again on the edge of his bed. He could hear his sisters, Jody and Sarah, in their room at the end of the hall, talking to each other's dolls in the dolls' high-pitched voices. From the kitchen below, drifting up the narrow stairs as if wrapped in a parka, came the muffled, serious voice of the radio newscaster, and the click of Alvin's mother's shoes against the linoleum as she walked back and forth between the stove and the table where, he knew, his father sat smoking, rattling yesterday's paper, poking around in it for something he might have missed last night after supper.

Alvin thought, They all seem so innocent and so peaceful—Jody and Sarah quietly playing some domestic make-believe game with their dolls, Pa reading, waiting for his breakfast, eager to get to work, and Ma already at work, up since six, for God's sake, eggs collected, chickens watered and fed, breakfast for the rest of us under way. Compared to them, his wonderful family, he was a beast. And none of them knew it—though he thought maybe his father suspected.

Ordinarily, he liked listening to the sounds of his family and thinking about those four people as a single unit. But this morning, when he thought of them, he was so aware of their collective purity and strength, their communal innocence, that he was forced back upon the images of his own solitary corruption and weakness, his steadily accumulating guilt. Over and over, the images of how he had behaved the night before, first in the boys' bathroom at the high school and then later in Feeney's car and after that in the cottage at the lake, took detailed, vivid shapes in front of him, bringing him back to the facts of himself, the pollution he had become.

He had driven over to Pittsfield after supper with Chub Feeney and Roland Bilodeau, his closest friends, to help decorate the gym for Saturday's dance, the annual "Spring Bacchanal," as it had been named by Miss Waite, the senior English teacher, and the student members of the dance committee. After stapling and taping crepe paper strips and balls for an hour or so, disguising the basketball backboards and free-throw zones at either end of the hall as "sacred groves," Feeney and Bilodeau had gone out to Leo's, to buy Cokes and hamburgers for the three of them and Mr. Fitch, too, the janitor who, earlier, had let the boys into the darkened, otherwise deserted building.

After a few seconds of chat about the weather (cold) Mr. Fitch had trudged down the basement stairs to his boiler-room hideout, and Alvin had found himself unexpectedly restless and alone. He stood in the middle of the brightly lit gym, a bear-sized boy already larger than most full-grown men, and then, without a single thought, machine-like, he strode out to the dark, locker-lined corridor, turned right, took about twenty long strides, turned right again, and entered the boys' bathroom.

It was completely dark, like the inside of a mattress, and smelled of ammonia and old cigarettes and disinfectant. Alvin closed his eyes tightly, scattering shards of light against the black screen behind his eyelids, moved unhesitatingly a few feet to his left and entered the second in a bank of six stalls, swinging the door closed behind him. With his eyes still jammed shut, he dropped his trousers and pulled down his jockey shorts and sat down on the cold toilet seat. Then, as if of its own volition, his stiffened penis jumped into his right palm. His hand, also acting on its own, closed around the thing and started yanking on it, working quickly and not very smoothly, as if trying vainly to get the owner's attention. The owner's attention, however, was elsewhere, was a few inches from the bulging cheeks of Dotty Cush, the well-known school slut, as his cock slipped into her mouth, was biting kind Miss Waite's milky shoulder as his cock plunged into her bushy pussy, was watching the beautiful and pure Betsy Cooper grimace with painful ecstacy as she took his cock into her asshole, when it splashed its semen into the cold toilet water, and he blinked open his eyes and, in the total darkness, saw where he was and what he was doing there.

Slowly, he zipped himself up, flushed the toilet, and walked back to the gym, where he sat down, on Bacchus' throne in the sacred grove, stared blankly across at Diana's throne in the grove opposite, and waited for his friends to return with the Cokes and hamburgers.

They swung through the door, grinning widely, and for a second Alvin thought, Oh my God, they were hiding in the next stall and they *know!* They *heard* me! But that was impossible, he realized, impossible, as Feeney pulled a soggy hamburger and a Coke from a paper bag and passed them to him. Naw, impossible. His two friends were still grinning, however, and looking at one another as if they knew something he didn't.

"What's up?" he asked them, his voice cracking. "Why're you guys so happy? You get laid over at Leo's or something?"

Feeney put his face close to Alvin's and said in a raspy voice, "We got some *beer!*"

"No shit?"

"No shit."

"How, for Christ's sake?" Alvin stuffed his hamburger into his mouth and gulped at the Coke while Feeney described how drunk ol' Henry Davis had been when they caught him in the parking lot outside, pissing against one of Feeney's whitewalls, and how Feeney had at first threatened to beat the shit out of the old geezer, then had promised to let him go if he would pick up half a dozen quarts of beer for them. Henry had agreed happily, gratefully, and they had driven over to Danis' Superette with him between them in the front seat, where he had purchased the beer, after which they had dropped the old man off at the Bonny Aire, not forgetting to stop at Leo's on the way back for food and Cokes.

"You oughta eat something anyhow. Before you start drinkin'," Bilodeau said somberly, as Alvin finished off his hamburger.

In a half-hour, they had rushed through the rest of the decorating and had fled the gym for Feeney's battered ten-year-old Ford sedan outside in the parking lot.

"Where do you guys want to go, to do the drinkin'?" Alvin asked.

"Take it easy, Al, ol' buddy. We got all night," Feeney told him. "Crack me open one of them quarts, will ya, Rollie? I got me a thirst that won't quit!" He laughed and slammed the steering wheel rim with the heel of his meaty hand.

They sat in the parked car and in minutes had emptied one of the quart bottles. Then Feeney declared, "What we need tonight is *women!*"

Alvin and Bilodeau agreed. "Yeah," they said.

"Where?" asked Bilodeau from the back seat.

"Yeah, where?" repeated Alvin.

"Up at Alton. At the roller rink."

"Yeah?" Alvin said.

"Yeah. Two weeks ago I scarfed a broad from Prince Edward Island at that goddamn place. She had legs that almost broke my back, I ain't kiddin'. Yelled in French every fuckin' time she came," Feeney recalled, taking the last pull on the bottle, handing the empty over his shoulder to Bilodeau, who sat with the beer, the full bottles as well as the empties.

"I got a second cousin like that," Bilodeau said in a low, excited voice.

Alvin thought, I wish I was Catholic. I'd have had lots of girls by now if I was Catholic. He wasn't sure why or how it would make a difference, because he had stopped believing in Jesus altogether around the time he had stopped believing in Santa Claus. God, however, he still believed in, the way he believed in Goodness and Justice. He was positive, though, that if he been raised a Catholic, he would not still be a virgin. Sixteen years old and still a goddamn virgin. It was getting to be ridiculous. He was good-looking in a conventional way, smart ("Good in math," people said), and an athlete. He knew and admired these qualities in himself, and generally girls saw them and admired them, too. But he did not know a single Catholic boy his age who was similarly attractive and knew it, who was also a virgin. So it *had* to have something to do with being a Catholic. But what? Skinny little Feeney wasn't much to look at, for God's sake, though he was pretty smart and around women knew how to talk smooth. ("Feeney's *cute,*" they murmured.) And as for Bilodeau, he was a good-natured, two-hundred-pound hulk who looked like a buffalo and was about as dumb. ("Bilodeau's not too bright," they said, as if writing graffiti.) Yet neither Feeney nor Bilodeau had been virgins since they were thirteen years old.

At first, after having listened to lengthy, detailed descriptions of the several bodies the two boys had copulated with, Alvin had not believed them. But after a few months of it, he had decided that their tales were more than loosely based on actual persons and events, and then finally he believed them, even though it meant he had to be amazed by the two, as if they were sexual prodigies. Now,

however, three years later, it was his own sexual inexperience that
amazed him. The norm had been reversed. And now, of course,
there was this, this . . . *habit* of his. Yes, he was sure that, by not
having been born into a Catholic family, Alvin Stock had missed a
lot of life.

They were beyond Crawford, a few miles outside the town of Alton
Bay, where the roller rink was located. The car radio was at full
volume, and the disc jockey, honking and banging his manic way
along the air waves from Boston, two hours' drive away, had just
dropped "Earth Angel" by the Platters onto the turntable, and
Feeney was singing along sweetly as he drove. "Earth Angel, Earth
Angel, will you be mine? Love you forever, for all time . . ." They
were working on their fourth quart of beer. It was a clear, very cold
night, and the sky was stubbled with points of light. "I'm just a fool,
a fool in love with you-ooo."

Alvin reached over, turned down the radio, and tugged Feeney's
cuff. He said to him, "Listen, Feeney, I s'pose all the broads at this
place are French Canucks, right?"

"Wal, yeah, most of 'em. Quebec, P.E.I., the Maritimes, stuff
like that. You know. But *older,* man. Older women. In their *twen-
ties!"* He laughed and banged the steering wheel with his hand.

Alvin swallowed hard, ran his fingers back through his hair. "I
don't know, man, I mean . . . is that the kind of stuff we really
want? I mean, *really?"*

"Naw, we *really* want Marilyn Monroe. But how much chance you
got for getting some of that tonight?"

Alvin chugged his way through the remaining few inches of beer in
the bottle and passed the empty back to Bilodeau. Then, carefully,
after first apologizing to his good friend Bilodeau, assuring him that
he meant no offense to *him,* he went ahead and explained to his
good friend Feeney that he personally wasn't too hot about the idea
of screwing some twenty-five-year-old Frenchie. Not that screwing
somebody was such a big deal, you understand. It was just that,
well, for him, the idea kind of left him cold. Especially if they're
going to yell in French every time they come. Not that he didn't like

the French language, he assured Bilodeau, who was jumping around
in back on the floor looking for the package of Luckies he'd dropped.
Christ, no, he loved French, Alvin did, it was an extremely melodi-
ous language, and in fact he was vice-president of the French Club,
as Bilodeau knew, or at least he ought to know, if he cared about
who his friends were. And besides, what really bugged him was that
it was nine-thirty anyhow, so how were they going to get their boots
into three, or even *one,* of those broads in time to get back home to
Crawford before his old man, or Bilodeau's old man for that matter,
hit the goddamn ceiling?

Feeney didn't look over at him. "How long's it take you to make
it, lover boy?" he asked. Staring straight ahead, no longer smiling,
he drove into the town of Alton Bay, turned left at the blinking
yellow light in the center of the town, and headed along the bay.

That wasn't the point, Alvin explained, talking faster than before,
his voice raised a notch. No matter how fast they made it, they still
had to *talk* to them, for God's sake, they still had to get the dummies
into the car somehow and then drive off to the woods someplace
where they could screw them, even if they only got *one,* and then
they'd have to bring the damn broad back to where they got her in
the first place, and by that time it would be one or two in the morning, for Christ's sake, and they wouldn't get back to Crawford till at
least a half-hour after that, and they all remembered what his and
Bilodeau's fathers had done the last time they came in that late when
they were supposed to have been home at midnight, and tonight it
would be even worse, because they were supposed to be decorating
the goddamn gym and nothing else, so if his old man started phon-
ing around, if he called the school, say, and got old man Fitch on the
line, well, he for one didn't feel much like getting grounded for a
month or punched around by his old man either, and he figured
Bilodeau felt the same . . .

"Yeah," Bilodeau said, popping the cap off another quart of beer
with his pocketknife. "But I'll tell ya something, Al," he said dully.
"That shit about the French? I'll kick your ass, man, you make any
more cracks like that. We ain't niggers, you know."

Alvin said nothing.

"You *hear* me, man?" Bilodeau said, grabbing Alvin's shoulder from behind and yanking it back and forth.

"Yeah, I hear you. But it's hard to understand, with the accent," he answered, ducking Bilodeau's long, slow punch at his head. Then he spun his body around, was up on his knees in the front seat, reached into the darkness, and, with his right fist, punched his friend full in the face, following with a left and another right, twice. Bilodeau grabbed his arms and started pulling on them at the elbows, and, while the two grunted, swore, pulled, and thrashed between the seats, Feeney frantically yelled at them and pulled the car over to the side of the road.

"You stupid sons of bitches!" Feeney was screaming. "Get the hell outta my car if you wanna fight!" He jumped out and ran around to Alvin's side, opened the door, and pulled on his legs, dragging him out of the car to the ground.

Bilodeau scrambled over the seatback after him and in a second stood outside over him, shaking with rage, blood streaming from his nose. "I'll kill ya! I'll kill ya!"

Alvin rolled over on his back, flopped his arms out, and smiled up at his friend. Then he laughed.

They drove north past the roller rink, a low, barn-like wooden structure with a large parking lot on three sides and the lake behind it. Then, after driving about a mile along the curving, narrow road, they turned right and bumped along a dirt road that ended in the center of a cluster of wood-frame summer cottages at the edge of the lake. The still surface of the water glistened coldly in front of the car.

"If you'da shut up a minute back there, I coulda told you about this place," Feeny said to Alvin, who was in the back now, alone, curled up like a question mark and giggling.

"You know Betsy Cooper?" Feeney continued. "Her old man's the one who owns these cottages. All of 'em. He rents the little ones an' keeps the big one there for his own family from June to Labor Day. It's like a goddamn hotel inside. Wait'll you see it, you guys ain't gonna believe this place," he promised. "Asshole there was worried about where we was going to get our pussy," he said, jabbing his thumb towards Alvin in the back. "I been comin' here all *winter*, man," he said with disdain.

He shut off the motor, and the three boys got out of the car and lurched in darkness towards the house. It was a small, well-kept, cedar-shingled colonial with a screened porch that ran around all four sides. Feeney led the way, Bilodeau carried the remaining quart and a half of beer, and Alvin stumbled along behind.

"Hey!" Alvin yelled. "Where the fuck *are* we? Whayda-fuck-ah-wee? You guys ever hear of the whayda-fuck-ah-wee bird? Whay-dafuckahwee! Whaydafuckahwee!" he squawked, flapping his arms and looping over the lawn in clumsy circles. "They were named after the lost Whaydafuckahwee Indian tribe!" he bellowed.

"*Will you shut up!*" Feeney hissed from the door. He leaned over the lock and sprung the latch with his pocketknife, swung the door open and walked confidently into the living room, as if his father and not Betsy Cooper's owned the place. "There's a candle on the fireplace mantle," he said, walking knowledgeably in the darkness across the room to the fireplace.

Holding the candle low, he lit it, and the room filled with vague, flickering light. "Only thing, we gotta be careful that when we leave everything's the same as when we came," he warned. "Like I said, I been coming here all winter and nobody's caught on to it yet." He walked casually to the thermostat on the pine-paneled wall and switched on the furnace. "No sense in freezing our asses off," he said to no one in particular. Then, to Bilodeau, who stood in the center of the large room: "C'mon, man, I'll show you where the bathroom is, so you can wash the blood off your fucking face. You look like shit. Bring the candle," he ordered, and the two of them, carrying the candle and beer with them, left Alvin alone, seated in the suddenly dark room crosslegged on the floor in front of the cold fireplace.

Morose now, alone in the darkness and surrounded by the bulky shapes of furniture covered with sheets, with no clear idea of where he was (except that he was in a house that was owned by Betsy Cooper's father), feeling dizzy and a little nauseous from the beer, he thought, It could've been horrible if we'd picked up a woman at that place. I wouldn't have had *anything* for her. Not now. Not so soon, after what I did with it . . . back there, at school. I know it, I'm sure of it. Wasted, thrown away, gone, millions and millions of sperms. A sea of them. Not enough time to make any more. I would've been empty. Thank God I talked them out of it. What a lousy way to get your first fuck. Who needs it? Really, *who?* Not that way. Not this way.

After a few minutes, the others came back and joined him on the floor, Bilodeau jamming the candle into the neck of an emptied beer bottle. Quietly chatting, relaxed now, the boys passed the remaining two bottles back and forth for a while, until the beer was finished. Bilodeau yawned, stretched, suggested they leave. It was eleven o'clock.

"Wait a minute," Alvin said. "I gotta take a piss. Where's the fuckin' bathroom?"

"Down the hall to the end and at the left," Feeney told him. "Listen, don't touch anything, an' be sure you flush the fuckin' toilet, man. Whyn't you piss outside, anyhow? I don't want ol' man Cooper knowing that he's got some winter tenants, you know what I mean?"

Alvin told him to stuff it up his ass, and he moved carefully down the hall carrying the candle in the bottle.

The bathroom was large and elaborately decorated with pink fixtures and a purple wall-to-wall carpet. Alvin looked down at the carpeting and giggled. Then he strode straight to the edge of the large pink bathtub, took down his trousers and undershorts, sat on the cold edge of the tub and shat into its emptiness. He wiped himself with a purple handtowel, buckled his pants, flushed the toilet as he passed it, and quickly walked back into the living room. "Let's go," he told his friends. "My ol' man's gonna have my ass if I don't get home before twelve."

His father stood at the bottom of the stairs, shouting up to him. "Alvin! For Christ's sake! It's seven-thirty!"

"Okay, Pa," he mumbled. The sound of his own voice sickened

him. It was still the voice of someone he loathed, an enemy.

Trudging down the stairs, however, dropping his weight onto every step as if his body were a sandbag, he suddenly, unexpectedly, imagined a way out—a way to defeat his enemy. It was, of course, the simplest way, almost simple minded, certainly simplistic. Nevertheless, by the time he reached the bottom of the stairs, he had decided. He would turn over a new leaf.

A new leaf. The phrase tumbled energetically through his mind, like a mountain stream filled with snowmelt, fresh and clean and irresistible. The way he saw it, as he sat down at the kitchen table for breakfast, the offending self was the outer self, not the inner, and therefore all he had to do was alter the outer self—his behavior.

Right? he asked himself. Right, he answered, knifing through a stack of pancakes. He would make five promises to himself. The first was never to masturbate again. For as long as he lived, he swore, as he popped a crisp stick of bacon into his mouth. The second promise was never to touch another drop of beer, or any other alcoholic beverage—at least until he was twenty-one, when he could do so legally. And after that, for the rest of his life, he would drink moderately, he pledged, draining the last of his first cup of coffee and holding it out to his mother so that she could refill it. The third was never to strike another human being. Never. He would become an out-and-out pacifist, working as a medic or ambulance driver if he got drafted and had to go to Korea or someplace where there was a war on. And he would never hit a friend of his, no sir, no matter how angry he got, and not even if that friend goaded him into it by kidding him because he was still a virgin, he promised, and polished off the rest of the pancakes, mopping up the syrup on his plate with a piece of buttered toast. The fourth pledge he made was always to respect women, even if it meant he had to remain a virgin until his wedding night. His fifth promise, made while carrying his dishes to the sink for his mother to wash, was always to respect private property.

"Today," his father said to him, "I want you to count fittings." Gaunt and grim, his grimness harshened by his straight, finger-thin moustache, the man stood by the door, pulling his coat on. He explained to his son that he needed an inventory of all his pipe and fittings, so he'd know what to order for the coming summer's work. "It's a simpleton's job, so you shouldn't screw it up if you concentrate and do exactly as I'm telling you," he said without smiling.

Alvin stared down at his feet and waited for instructions.

Handing him a pad of lined and columnar ruled paper and a pencil, his father told him how to indicate the types, sizes and quantities of the thousands of plumbing fittings that lay in bins in the barn. "It's going to take you more than a couple of weekends to get it done, so for Christ's sake don't get careless and lose your place, or else you'll have to start over again from the beginning. And since I'm paying you by the hour, I don't expect you to have to do anyting twice."

"Yeah," Alvin said. "Don't worry."

"Count all the cast iron fittings first. Then the copper. Then the I.P.S. brass. Then all the I.P.S. galvanized and black metal. And for Christ's sake, don't get them mixed together! Use a separate sheet of paper for each type of fitting, and write it here at the top. This is the first one, it says, 'C.I.—San. Tee.' You know what that means?" he asked sarcastically.

"Cast iron sanitary tee."

"That's right. The vertical columns are numbered to indicate the size of the run. Each tee has three sizes. You know how to read a tee, don't you?" he said in a flat voice.

"Yes."

"How?"

"Clockwise."

"Right. Don't screw it up. I'll be back this afternoon to check on you." Then, as gruffly but without sarcasm, he told his wife that he'd be in Concord at Capitol Supply for a while. He had a couple of small jobs to take care of over that way, too, some toilets needed a bit of reaming—"So if there's any calls, tell them I'll get back to them late this afternoon." Then he pulled his cap onto his head, turned and went out the door.

Alvin listened to his father's truck start up and drive out to the road, and, when he could no longer hear it, he put on his coat and gloves, picked up the pad and pencil from the table, and went out the door towards the barn. Crossing the backyard, which was covered with a hard, yellowish crust of old snow, he started whistling "Earth Angel", and then, after a few bars, lapsed into silence. It was a cold, high-overcast morning with a flat white sky that drained everything of color, casting in a shade of grey the spruce and pine trees, the unpainted barn, the sheds, even the house itself, a white Cape with an attached el. A light wind blew from the northeast, carrying the chilled cries of a pair of crows whose shapes Alvin could just make out against the snow-covered hilly fields near the horizon, a high half-mile beyond the second-growth conifers and birches that had started taking over his father's fields twenty years ago, when the man had quit farming and had become a plumber. The scrubby pines and birch groves now practically surrounded the house and outbuildings.

Walking into the barn, he flicked a light switch by the door and strolled along the facing rows of fitting bins to the far end, where he placed his pad and pencil on top of a keg of finish nails and started to count two-inch cast iron sanitary tees.

In a half-hour he had gotten up to four-inch cast iron sanitary tees, and he had realized that, try as he might, he was not capable of turning over a new leaf, for, moments before, he had decided that as soon as he finished counting the six-inch cast iron sanitary tees, he was going to take a break and was going to run into the house to get warmed by the kitchen stove, and then he was going to go upstairs to his bedroom to masturbate. Also, he had decided that tonight, if Feeney and Bilodeau were willing, he would drive up to Alton Bay with them and try to pick up some French Canadian girls at the roller rink, and, if he could, he'd try to take the girls to Betsy Cooper's father's summer cottage (he figured, without feeling even a twinge of guilt, that he'd rush into the bathroom and clean it up before the others had a chance to see what, in his drunken belligerence, he had done there). And too, he had decided that one of these days he and Bilodeau were going to have it out—they were the two largest boys in the school, the only ones not really frightened by the other's size—and he knew Bilodeau well enough to predict, after last night, a series of pushing, challenging encounters between them that would have to culminate eventually in a full-blown fistfight. Besides, he said to himself, he was pretty sure he could take the Frenchman anyhow.

As if he were a person separated from himself, he watched himself making plans, scheming impatiently, plotting his own damnation. He felt bisected, or worse, as if he were two separate human beings rather than a single split one. And one of the two persons was the dreamer, the other the dreamed, and neither was capable of knowing for sure which was which. And while the one planned, schemed, and plotted, the other groaned in revulsion, dismay, and helplessness.

It struck him that he would not be so repulsed by himself if he didn't continually, daily, have to face his family, his friends, and all the other people in town who knew him and thought him to be pretty much the way he wanted to be. ("Alvin Stock is a fine young man," they all told each other.) His secret life, or at least the particular aspect of secrecy, depended upon the assumptions about him that were held by people who thought they knew him. Remove those assumptions, he reasoned, and he would go a long way towards removing the secrecy. He felt sure that it was the secrecy more than anything else that disgusted him. If thine right eye offend thee, pluck it out, he admonished himself. At any rate, he couldn't imagine being as deeply offended by his string of weaknesses if there just weren't so many people around who thought him free of those very weaknesses.

Sitting on the frozen dirt floor of the barn, he went on counting the fittings, but, as he counted (he was up to four-inch cast iron ninety-degree elbows), he pictured a life in which no one thought him free of weaknesses because no one knew him in the first place—a life peopled entirely with total strangers. He would pack a bag, one small suitcase would be enough, and after everyone had gone to bed, he would pop out from under his blankets fully clothed, and he would tiptoe down the stairs to the kitchen, where he would

leave a note, short, cryptic, for his mother, and he would be gone. The note, he decided, would say: *I've left to seek the company of strangers. By my weakness, I've been denied a new leaf. I'm choosing, therefore, a new life. Don't worry about me. I'll be in touch as soon as I've relocated myself. Or I should say, "located,"* he added ironically. He signed it with just his initial, *A*. Then he added a *P.S. Tell Jody and Sarah that I love them and will miss them, especially their innocent voices as they play together with their dolls in the morning. And, Pa, thanks for trying so hard to help me become a man. Maybe you've succeeded more than you thought. You always said it takes a man to face up to himself, his strengths and his weaknesses. And that's what I'm trying to do now. I'm sorry I didn't finish the inventory before I left. Maybe Roland Bilodeau will work for you as a helper, now that I'm gone. He mentioned last week that he was looking for a part-time job, and he's often told me that he wants to become a plumber or electrician after high school. I don't think I'm cut out for it anyhow, which is why I probably always made so many mistakes. And, Ma, even though my leaving probably hurts you a lot, please know that in the long run it'll make you happier. I'd only shame you if I stayed on in Crawford. No, I'm not the person you think I am. The details don't matter. Just take my word for it. It's better for everyone this way.*
Love, your son, Alvin.

Stepping from the warm darkness of the house into the cold darkness outside, closing the door silently behind him, he studied the stars for a few moments and started walking the dirt road towards Crawford Center, two miles west, and the north-south highway, Route 28, beyond. He walked past the darkened houses in which, he knew, his and his family's friends and neighbors had slept peacefully for all their lifetimes. Goodbye to the Youngs, he said, as he passed the yellow bungalow next to the Congregational Church. Goodbye to the Pinkhams, the Feeneys, the Cates, the Eastmans. Goodbye to the Bilodeaus, the Bouchards, the Riviers. Goodbye to Crawford, New Hampshire, and, yes, goodbye to Alvin Stock, too, he said to himself as he plodded along the side of the one road that ran through the town. Your native son has left, and he's taken with him as little of himself as possible.

It's not unlikely that his eyes were moist with tears as he stepped up to the shoulder of Route 28 and stuck out his thumb to the first truck that came cruising down the highway all the way from Quebec, headed for Boston with a load of freshly milled wide pine boards. The truck came to a stop a hundred yards down the road and waited, lights blinking invitingly, as Alvin ran down the road to it and scrambled into the warm, cozy cab.

From that moment on, his eyes were never again dimmed with tears, because at that moment Alvin Stock had become a man.

In New Orleans he signed on as a deckhand for one of the shrimp boats. Thanks to his two years of French at Pittsfield High, plus a native facility with languages ("Alvin Stock was *always* good in languages!"), he mastered the Cajun dialect in a matter of weeks and thus was quickly able to earn the trust of the crews and masters of the shrimp boats. And because of his unusual size and strength, his natural physical skills and his easy-going yet competitive temperament, he just as swiftly earned the respect of those suspicious, cliquish rogues. In a month, or even less, he was accepted as one of them—and by some was regarded as a leader.

He wore a tattoo of a bearpaw (after having been nicknamed "Ze Yankee Bear" by the seamen) the size of a quarter on the back of each hand. A Cajun girl named Mantilla—with pierced ears, ebony hair, green eyes that flashed like emerald fire, delicate pear-shaped breasts, dusky skin, passions born in the bayous and a tenderness learned from her slave-born grandmother—fell in love with him.

There were long nights of drinking rum with brawny, dark-skinned fishermen who carried razor-sharp knives and fought each other good naturedly in dockside taverns. There was a cynical but wise and good-hearted compadre named Pierre, a small, wiry man in his late forties who walked with a limp and whose wrinkled yet twinkling face was marked by long, jagged scars, remnants of ancient battles in nameless bars in famous ports.

Then, on a late summer voyage off the Yucatan, aboard the *Baton Rouge,* a hurricane struck, and the captain and his mate were washed overboard, and Alvin took command. He brought back the boat, crew, and a record catch, all intact, and the owners immediately offered him a boat of his own, the chance to be the youngest and most respected captain on the waterfront.

He declined, giving no reason, and the next morning he was gone, vanished without a trace. Mantilla wept bitterly, and Pierre, comforting her, said: "Ah, zat one, 'e left ze way 'e came. Lak de wind from de nord, a man wiz no past iz a man wiz no future. 'e was what 'e seemed to be, eh? No more, no less. Ah, be tankful, ma petite Mantilla. For 'e did not *lie* to you."

He'd worked his way through the cast iron fittings and now was counting half-inch copper couplings, grabbing five at a time by sticking his left hand into the bin and inserting his four fingertips and thumb into the ends of the couplings, plucking them out of the bin, as if his fingertips were magnetized and the couplings made of iron, releasing them with a flick of his hand into a pile shaped roughly like a pyramid at his feet. With every shake of his left hand, he wrote ⊞ on the pad with his right. He had made this mark, for couplings alone, several hundred times now and had lost all sense of quantity, was not even slightly aware of what he was doing, except that he knew he was functioning efficiently and with accuracy.

A chill had entered and taken up residence at the center of his body. Starting at his feet and hands, working slowly up the lengths of his extremities, it finally had settled in an area just behind and below his shoulder blades, above his kidneys and below his heart. He thought of palm trees softly clattering in a tropical breeze, open windows along the cobbled streets of the French Quarter, fruit vendors in shirtsleeves selling fresh melons, grapefruits, mangoes, and pineapples. And then he thought of the chunk of ice that had lodged at the center of his body. Putting the inventory pad and the pencil on the ground next to the pile of copper couplings, he stuffed his numbed hands into his jacket pockets and decided that his dream of "a new life" was just that, a dream, nothing more, useless to him, a trick he was playing only on himself. It was the dreamer deceiving the dreamed again.

No, he was who he was—both the dreamer *and* the dreamed, regardless of who could know it, regardless of whether or not the people around him saw no difference between the two. He was stuck with it, and, wherever he ran, he would have to bear both his selves along. New Orleans, the French Quarter, drinking and fighting with old Pierre, lying beside his beloved Mantilla—he'd still remain the dark and scheming, lascivious, self-profaning dreamer and dreamed. There simply was no way for him to flee that burden.

He started walking towards the house, hunched over, hands fisted in pockets, feet crunching against the hardened snow. It was eleven-thirty. By the time he got rid of the chill, his lunch would be ready for him. He wouldn't have to return to the counting again until twelve-thirty, he thought with bitter pleasure. As he walked along, he thought, One thing I *could* do is the one thing I've never *dared* to try. Get rid of the me who dreams, the one whom everyone admires and has such high hopes for. Become openly the person whose life so far has been such a deep secret. Just go ahead and walk around playing with myself, jack off every chance I get, drink myself drunk every chance I get, screw everything that'll let me, beat the shit out of anyone who gets in my way—in short, become in public the very person I already am in private. Then at least no one could accuse me of pretending to be someone I'm not, he reasoned.

The bastards. They'd be getting the real thing, the genuine article. They'd shut their mouths then, all right. All that talk about Dartmouth and going to college and "My, wouldn't your parents be pleased?" All that crap. At least *that* would be over. Miss Waite wouldn't dare look up from her desk. Too afraid I'd have a hard-on poking through my pants right at her batting eye. Dottie Cush would start to hang around my locker. "When can I give ya a handjob, Alvin?" And that Betsy Cooper—she'd be calling *me* on the phone, instead of some twerp in pre-med in Washington, D.C. She'd be saying, "Next time my parents take off for a weekend to ski, why don't you drop by and help me with my French, Alvin?" "No," I'd say to her, "you just meet me up at your parents' cottage at the lake. Bring candles." And if Feeney didn't like me cutting in on his territory, I'd grab the skinny bastard by the throat and put him against the wall in school, right in front of everybody, teachers and everyone else, and I'd say, "Listen, Feeney, when you're big enough to tell me where I can fuck my girl and where I can't, *then* you do it. But not now, little man. You still aren't big enough for that." And if Pa started yelling at me when I was working for him, calling me stupid again, I'd turn on the bastard and tell him to find himself a nigger to yell at, because I ain't going to be his nigger anymore. Not for sixty-five cents an hour. Not a buck twenty-five. Not for anything. The bastard. Let him count his goddamn fittings himself. I'll get a job pumping gas at McAllister's or something, just enough money to buy beer and maybe save up enough to buy a car, buy Feeney's old Ford, maybe, and every night buy some beer and drive up to Alton Bay and pick up some French broad at the roller rink and drive out to old man Cooper's cottage with her and screw her till the fucking sun comes up.

That's what all those bastards deserve. And I'd be doing them a favor, actually, letting them see the truth for once, letting them know who I really am by getting rid of the me who runs around hiding the other me, the me who smiles and talks so sweetly and intelligently with teachers, who is so "reasonable" and "mature," who is peaceable, sober, disciplined, a hard-working credit to his "poor but honest" parents, who eagerly helps his father in a failing one-man plumbing business by working weekends and summers for less money than a stranger would get, who honors his mother by never having anything to do with a girl he cannot bring home to have supper at his mother's table.

And I'd be giving *myself* exactly what *I* deserve, too. I'd be doing myself a big favor, because I'd be getting rid of the whiner, the complainer, the guilty conscience. I'd be silencing the nigger, the harpy, the worried one, kissing off the frightened one, the shy one, the insecure one. Because that's the one, in his public clothes, that everybody has such high hopes for. That's the one the girls tell their problems to but never offer handjobs to, the one my father walks over, the one my mother brags about at her sewing circle, the one the French Canadian girls wouldn't touch with a ten-foot pole . . .

He ate lunch quickly in sullen silence, ignoring his mother's cheerful attempts to engage him in conversation. "What's the matter,

Alvin?" she finally asked. "Don't you feel well?" She walked to the table where he sat eating his tuna fish sandwich and placed the cool, smooth palm of her hand against his forehead. "You have a fever, Alvin. You shouldn't be working out there in that cold barn. You'll catch your death of cold out there, son."

He pulled his head away from her hand as if he were dodging a blow. "I'm all right," he said. "Besides, you think I'm going to explain to Pa how I couldn't work today because you said I had a cold? Forget it," he gruffly advised her, going back to his sandwich.

"I don't know. I just don't know. Sometimes I just wonder about all that . . ." Her hands fluttered nervously about each other like a pair of sparrows.

"Well, don't." He got up from the chair, poked his arms into his coatsleeves, and stomped outside.

Returning to the barn, he squatted on the ground next to the pile of half-inch copper couplings and went on with the counting.

After a while, finished with the couplings, he dumped them back into the bin and started on the elbows, as before, grabbing them five at a time with the thumb- and fingertips of one hand, dropping the five onto the floor with a shake, then making his mark on the inventory pad. The only sounds were the regular clinks as he threw the fittings to the ground, occasionally the high, light cackling of the hens in the henhouse, and the distant calls of crows from the fields. And gradually, as he worked through the afternoon, his anger against his friends and his parents and their friends abated, to be replaced, slowly, one cell at a time, with feelings for them that approached sorrow, sorrow for their ignorance of him, for their apparent affection, respect, and even, in some cases, their admiration of him. He felt sorrow for their having such hopes that, he now knew, he could never fulfill. And so, naturally, he thought of suicide.

He heard his father's truck drive up and stop by the house, heard the kitchen door slam. He had used up nearly half the inventory pad—all the cast iron fittings and most of the copper had been counted. Because they were both small and numerous, the copper fittings had taken the most time, though not as much as he'd anticipated. He was a third of the way down the first of the two walls of bins, considerably further along than he'd expected to be by this time.

He looked at his watch. Three-thirty. One hour to go. Then he looked down at the fitting in his hand—a one-inch threaded brass tee. The sheet on the pad in front of him, however, insisted that he was now counting one-inch *copper* tees, with sweat ends, not threaded, and, worse, the dozen sheets before it indicated that he had been counting one-inch copper fittings for some time now. He checked the dozen bins before the one in front of him, and he found that he had been counting one-inch *brass* fittings for some time now, not copper.

Then he remembered, earlier, counting half-inch copper fittings *out* of the bins, piling them onto the floor, and, when the bin was both emptied and its contents counted, scooping the fittings off the floor and pitching them back in—until this afternoon, when he had reversed the order by dumping the fittings onto the floor first, then counting and replacing them as he counted.

He realized that at some point, therefore, he must have altered his procedure without knowing it, possibly halfway through whatever bin of fittings he happened to have been counting when he stopped for lunch. This meant that, by reversing his moves at midday, he had miscounted at least one size and type of fitting, and, worse, he had been counting brass for copper for at least twelve whole bins. Therefore, he concluded, the entire inventory could not be trusted. If he had messed up twice without being aware of it at the time, only by accident finding out now, then he had probably messed up numerous times and would never find out—until it was too late, until one June morning when his father, sending him to the barn for fifty one-inch copper elbows, would have to be informed that there are no more one-inch copper elbows in the bin. His father will say, Gee, the inventory you made in March shows that there are over three hundred left, and Alvin will have to answer, Gosh, Pa, there don't seem to be any left at all.

Still squatting on the frozen ground, he heard the sound of coarse cloth behind him, and, turning on one heel, he saw his father standing over him, hands in jacket pockets, cigarette held tightly between thin lips, humorless blue eyes looking past the son at the yellow pad on the ground. "Done?" he asked Alvin. "No need to sit around here putting in your time if you're all done." He was joking, Alvin knew.

"No-o," Alvin said, his voice cracking into a yodel.

His father leaned down and picked up the pad, studying it for a few seconds.

One of the roosters started his cock-a-doodle-doo and, halfway through it, abruptly broke off.

"The bastards can't be hungry. Ma fed 'em this morning," Alvin said uselessly.

"Yeah," his father said. "You're fucking this up, you know. Counting I.P.S. brass and writing copper sweat."

"I know." Alvin stared at the brass fittings in the bin next to him, hating them, despising their round, threaded mouths, their crusty yellow skins, their inappropriate weight. "I just this minute found out."

"Jee-sus Christ!"

"Sorry."

"Who knows what else you've fucked up? Do *you?*"

"No, Well, yes, sort of. I have to count the half-inch copper elbows over again, I think," Alvin said in an empty voice.

"You *think.*"

"Yes."

His father walked down to the bin that held the half-inch copper elbows and stared into the bin at the eight or nine hundred macaroni-shaped fittings. Then, in a low voice, "So you *think* you fucked these up, too, do you?"

"Yes. Maybe not, though."

"Jee-sus! And you're supposed to be the *smart* one! Well, I'm not supposed to be anything but a plumber, but it sure as shit looks to me like you gotta count every damn fitting in this place over again. Right from the beginning. Is that how it looks to you—since you're the *smart* one?"

"Yes."

"And tell me this, Mister Smartass. If you've gotta do everything over again, am I supposed to *pay* you for what you've already done today? Am I supposed to pay you for fucking up?"

Alvin glared up at his father's face. "No. You're not supposed to pay me for fucking up. I do that for nothing," he said grimly.

"You bet your ass you do," his father said, tossing the inventory pad on the ground in front of him and stalking out of the barn.

Hanging might suffice. There is always that dramatic moment when they discover the body swaying limply, casting its long shadow against the wall. He remembered seeing a hundred-foot coil of thick manila rope in the toolroom. He looked up into the darkened eave of the barn and saw that he could get to one of the high rafters by pulling a ladder into the loft with him and climbing from there. Inching his way along the center rafter, until he reached the midpoint, directly over the bay where he was now sitting solidly on the ground, he could tie the rope tightly to the beam, crawl back to his ladder, and descend to the loft again, where he could stand and make the noose. Then he could slip it over his head and, walking to the edge of the loft, could simply drop his body into space, as if down a well, and, swinging slowly between the bins, his neck broken, his body running out of air, he would die. Easy. A snapped neck, then unconsciousness, and finally strangulation. Once his neck was broken, the rest was painlessly simple. Assuming, of course, that he lost consciousness when his neck broke. But he knew he would. It wouldn't be a slight break, not with his weight, and not from that height. He'd be lucky if he didn't yank his head right off, he thought, shuddering.

When would he do it? Not now. Not enough time. In another hour supper would be ready. And after supper there was the dance at school, the "Spring Bacchanal." He'd like to see his friends one more time, for the sake of the few innocent and, therefore, happy days he'd spent with them in the distant past. They would all say, "But I saw ol' Al last night at the dance, and he was as cheerful and friendly as ever! Who would've thought there was such suffering and sadness inside good ol' Al?"

After the dance he would do it. Late, after coming home and

saying good night to his mother, who, as usual, would have waited up for him. He would lie in bed, fully clothed, waiting until he knew she was asleep, and then he'd jump out of bed and, flashlight in hand, head for the barn. He would pin a note to his shirt: *Ma, I love you too much to disappoint you the way I've disappointed myself. Pa, I know with you the disappointment has already begun, because in some ways you know me better than anyone else does. Jodie and Sarah, I love you and am sorry that I won't be able to listen to your innocent laughter at play anymore. —Alvin.* He would write the note tonight, after he got home from the dance and had gone upstairs, ostensibly to bed. He'd have to remember to take a safety pin out to the barn with him, so he could pin the note to his shirt. He knew there weren't any safety pins in the barn, and he'd sure feel silly if, after he'd got the rope up, he had to come back to the house to look for one. This was the one thing in his life he wanted to be sure he got right the first time.

At supper he was polite, even decorous, and, although somewhat distant, kind. He helped his mother serve the creamed peas and haddock to his sisters, smiling attentively into each face as he ladled out the food.

To his father he was deferential, restrained, speaking only when spoken to and then speaking precisely and to the point. His father asked him if he intended to go out tonight, and Alvin answered simply, in a pleasant monotone, "Yes, sir, to a school dance." He felt centered, balanced. A rare and wonderful feeling.

"Who's driving?"

"Chub Feeney."

"Feeney, eh? No drinking."

"Yes, sir."

"Home by midnight."

"Yes, sir."

When the meal was over, Alvin excused himself from the table and went upstairs to dress and, he had decided, to shave his whiskers. He had shaved seventeen times in his life so far, and this winter he'd reached the point where he was shaving once every three weeks, approximately.

He enjoyed the fact that he was now old enough to shave, but each occasion for it gave him a feeling of ambivalence, because afterwards his cherry-red cheeks and neck made him look to his eyes even more boyish than before he had shaved, when his lower face and neck had been covered with the fuzzy net of beginning whiskers. Thus the act that, for him, expressed his manhood served as well to disguise it and make him look more a boy.

Staring into the bathroom mirror at his face, he decided that tonight it wouldn't matter, that, actually, when they discovered his body, he preferred it to have a boyish rather than a mannish look. He lathered up his cheeks, chin, upper lip, and throat and began to scrape away the whiskers, careful not to bump and slice open any of the dozen or so pimples that had been spreading erratically across his lower face for the last three years. They were his permanent guests, just as unwelcome. No rudeness or kindness on his part could make them go away, and he finally had resigned himself to their presence, grateful, when he looked at the red, pocked, and constantly extruding faces of some of his friends, that it wasn't worse.

Finished, he slapped some sweet-smelling after-shave lotion against his cheeks and throat, wincing, but relishing the thick aroma just the same, despite the sudden, inevitable memory it evoked of his father, who used coarse bay rum, saying one morning as they climbed into the pickup together, "Jee-sus Christ, Alvin, you smell like a goddamn faggot!"

Then a dollop of Wildroot Creme Oil into the palm of his hand, and his usual observation, barely conscious, that it was the same quantity, consistency, and almost the color of a single ejaculation. He rubbed his hands together a few seconds, then massaged his scalp thoroughly and combed his hair, straight back, as always, without a part. Lately, his mother had been urging him to get a crewcut, but his friends, especially Feeney and Bilodeau, had been flaunting long, wet ducktails at him, so he had tried to keep everyone happy by combing his hair back severely straight and slick before he left the house, and, as soon as he was outside, sweeping the top and rear into what he hoped was a restrained, yet elegant, pompadour.

But tonight, he decided, there would be no pretense. No vain attempts to look "cool." He would be simply who he was, he promised himself.

He dressed quickly, noting with relief as he pulled on his clean khaki pants that he hadn't masturbated once today, even though several times he had wanted to. Then, as he pulled his charcoal grey crew-neck sweater over a white shirt, he saw in his dresser mirror that the collar of the shirt, poking a half-inch above the neck of the sweater, made him look like a minister, one of those youthful, liberal ministers who are skilled at sports like tennis and touch football and are supposed to be sympathetic to the problems of young people—but when he saw that, he realized with red-faced shame that anyone who takes pride in having gone a day without masturbating is a disgusting human being.

He sat silently in the back seat of the car, while Feeney and Bilodeau in front, high spirited, snapping fingers to the beat of the songs on the radio, chewing gum, smoking cigarettes, smelling of hair lotion and cologne and deodorant and woolen clothes, yelled—at Alvin, at the radio, at each other, at the car, out the closed windows at the cold spring night.

"Whoo-whee! Thank God it's fucking Saturday!"

"*Pussy*-day!"

"Oh, oh-hh, oh, oh, oh-hh, *yeah,* oh *yeah,* man, I got me a case of lover's nuts that won't fucking quit! *You* drive, *you* drive, man! I gotta hold onto my *balls!*"

"How 'bout you, Stock? Whassamatta with you, man? What you doin' back there in the dark, ol' buddy, playin' with your peter?"

"Pullin' on your pud?"

"Massagin' your meat?"

"Pumpin' your prick?"

"Beatin' the bishop?"

"Whackin' your whang?"

"Diddlin' your dong?"

"Hey, man, I don't care what you do with it, but for Christ's sake, man, don't fuck up my *upholstery* with it!"

Alvin said nothing. It was seven miles from Crawford to the high school in Pittsfield, and if Feeney or Bilodeau noticed his sustained silence during the trip, neither of them bothered to mention it. He was grateful for their tact, or insensitivity. Whichever, it didn't matter. He knew that if one of them asked what was the matter, he wouldn't be able to explain truthfully, and yet he couldn't lie. He couldn't think of a lie to tell. The fact almost amazed him. It was the first time in his life that he remembered being unable to think of a lie. He was at that peculiar point where he knew that he had no choice but, if asked, to answer with the truth. Regardless of how it got understood. Every time he thought, Oh, well, if one of them says anything, I'll just tell him . . . , his mind filled with a black, syrupy substance which dissipated as soon as the truth started trickling in: I'm silent tonight, guys, because I've decided to kill myself tonight. Not because life isn't worth living, guys, but because *I'm* not worth living. I guess you could call it an execution, actually. Or a kind of mercy killing . . .

All the way to Pittsfield.

He felt physically strange, too, as if his decision had somehow altered his metabolism. He was shaking, shivering with cold. The small of his back felt knotted and icy. His limbs felt cumbersome, sodden, thick and graceless, and his whole head felt swollen, puffed out around his eyes and mouth, so that it seemed he was looking and talking, when he talked, down a tunnel. He felt trapped inside his skin, but only tentatively, and explosively, the way a smoldering volcano is trapped by the earth's crust just before it erupts. He was a little frightened by the way things were going.

"I don't feel good," he heard himself say with an echo as the car pulled into the school parking lot.

Feeney shut the motor off and flipped off the headlights and, turning around in the warm interior darkness of the car, said in a raspy voice, "Wal, man, you done come to the right place, 'cause your old pal Feeney's got some *medicine* for you. Huh, Rollie, we got what Stock needs, don't we, man?"

Bilodeau laughed.

"Naw, that's okay, I feel okay, you guys."

"Uh-uh-uh-uh. Doctor Feeney just this minute heard you say you didn't feel good. I even know what the symptoms are, man."

"No, no kidding. I'm okay. Let's go in."

"Wait a minute, man, wait a minute. The symptoms. You're tense, nervous. Right?"

"Right. Let's go in, I'll be okay once I get in." Alvin moved for the door.

"No ya don't, man! You don't *feel* good, remember? You need some medicine, man. Don't ya wanta feel *good,* man?"

"I feel okay now. Honest."

Feeney twisted his face into a question mark. "You don't understand, Al, baby. Show him what we got, Rollie," he said. "Jesus, pal, you ain't too quick tonight."

Bilodeau went into the glove compartment with one huge hand and drew out a paper bag and pulled from the bag a pint of Canadian Club. He held it by the cap, dangling it proudly and slightly defiantly in front of Alvin's face, like a fish he had just caught. "Hard stuff!" he said happily.

"Hard stuff!" Feeney repeated expectantly.

"Hard stuff," Alvin said in a dead voice.

Bilodeau put the bottle back inside the bag and, after folding the bag carefully down to expose the neck of the bottle, unscrewed the cap and took a long slug from it. "Ah-h-h! *Shit,* man! Here, man," he said, handing the bottle to Feeney.

Feeney wiped the mouth of the bottle delicately with his tobacco-stained fingertips and took a slug, wiping his own mouth afterwards with his coatsleeve. *"Yeah!"* he wheezed. "This is goin' to be a fuckin'-A all right Saturday night."

"Yeah. Fuckin'-A," Bilodeau said.

Feeney handed the bottle over the back of the seat to Alvin. "Here you go, man. Here's the medicine I was talkin' about," he said sarcastically.

"No."

"What?"

"No."

"What're you talkin' about? It's *hard stuff!"*

"No."

"What? Are you some kinda asshole? Do you know what kinda shit I had to go through to get this? C'mon, drink!" Feeney ordered.

"No."

Bilodeau turned away and looked out the window beside him. "Fuck him. He's chickenshit."

"Yeah," Feeney said, disgusted. "G'wan inside, man. Your little schoolmates're waitin' for ya. Take off, man. Screw!"

"Yeah, screw, asshole!" Bilodeau said, not looking at him.

Silently, Alvin opened the door, stepped out to the parking lot, and walked away. He was moving his body as if it were a stranger's, deciding consciously with each step to lift one foot and place it down in front of the other. Aiming his body in the approximate direction of the door to the gym and the small crowd of people gathered there, he crossed the parking lot and arrived finally face to face with Miss Waite, who was standing just inside the door, greeting the students as they entered.

He still felt as if his metabolism had been somehow altered. His body was slow, heavy, awkward, cold—as if the force of gravity had been increased slightly. His face felt like a pillow attached to the front of his head, with small tubes placed for his eyes and mouth. He had no peripheral vision whatsoever, and his voice sounded to him first densely muffled and then hollow and echoing. Other people's voices seemed to be coming through a thin wall, as if they were talking to each other in an adjacent room. Foregrounds and backgrounds shifted erratically, and people moved by him one minute as if in slow motion, the next as if in doubletime. And he was oddly unafraid now.

Although most of the time he was forced to concentrate on getting himself physically from one place to another, he now and again was moved to reflect for an instant on his situation—to the effect that he already regarded himself as half-removed, as partially absent, from the life around him. He believed that it was literally true, so that if at this moment he were to be photographed, when the film was developed it probably would reveal only his outline, or maybe it would show him only as a grey, semi-transparent shadow.

Miss Waite's face, moon shaped, white, with a large red slash for a mouth, spiders for eyes, and a jagged corona of black hair surrounding it, loomed into view, gaily grimacing. Hell-OOO-o, Alvin, we were afraid you might not be coming! We need you, need you, need you here tonight, for the Court, you're in the Court, the Court of Dionysus. And the decorations, the decorations, the decorations look wonderful, wonderful, wonderful. A wonderful job, a job. I'll bet it was a job. Your hands are cold, so cold, it must be cold out tonight, such cold hands . . .

Past Miss Waite and into the gym, where, because the lights were low and because the crowd had not yet dispersed into the room, but had formed at the entrance in a bright clot of faces, sweaters, shirts, dresses, hair ribbons, neckties, he saw nothing but Dotty Clark, her apple-shaped face bobbing on top of bulging, powder-blue, sweatered breasts. Her arms and hands extended themselves towards him, like a pair of eels drifting underwater, and her large mouth opened wide. Her teeth, loose pink tissue behind lips, and her tongue were undulating slowly. Oh-h-h, Alvin Stock, it's ladies' choice so you have to dance, you *have* to dance, *you* have to dance, you have to *dance* with me, dance with *me,* let me give you a blow job, let me dance with *you,* you better not give me a snow job, I know you hate to dance but its ladies' choice . . . Smell of perfume, huge pink ear whorls, brown cloudy strands of hair against his forehead, and a voice, a girl's thin voice, from someplace behind him, below him and to his right, talking as if to someone else and from behind a screen about places, events, people he'd only heard about in half-forgotten rumors.

The music stopped, and he and the girl stopped moving, and he discovered that they were standing together in the middle of the room. A few couples were near them, but most of the people were lined up around the walls. The room itself was a huge, dimly lit hall, with an elaborately decorated throne set on a raised dais at each of the two ends of the hall. There was a group of five or six uniformed musicians standing on a platform midway along the third wall, with the entryway and Miss Waite midway along the fourth. The twin thrones and the areas immediately surrounding them were draped from someplace overhead near the ceiling down to the floor with green and gold leaf-covered gauze canopies that were illuminated from within by yellow and red electric lights that flickered as if they were torches, casting the thrones in a fiery light and throwing long, leaping shadows into the room

The music started again, and someone, a girl he knew but somehow could not identify to himself, grabbed his left hand with her right and, placing her left arm around him, started to dance him around in a circle. She talked rapidly, and he answered yes, yes, yes, in hisses, and no, no, no, until the music stopped again, when another girl he could recognize but not identify grabbed him, and when the music had resumed, this time with three of the musicians singing loudly into a microphone and the others playing on their instruments, they danced. The room was filled with dancers now, their bodies bumping carelessly against the calls and groans of the music.

At some point Alvin found himself dancing with a dark-haired girl he identified, with some measure of relief, as Betsy Cooper. Betsy Cooper! he said in a loud, echoing voice. Yes, she answered, and I'm glad you finally got around to asking me to dance, Mister Popularity, Mister Popularity, Mister Popularity! What're you trying to do, dance with every girl in school, every girl in school? I'm having a party, party, a party after the dance, just a few friends, a party, and I'd like you to come over to the party, party, party, won't you come to my party, party, party?

He was nodding down into her dark face and saying yes-ss-s, when the music stopped, a drum rolled, and Miss Waite, standing on the platform next to the musicians, called out to the crowd something that made them all applaud ferociously and cheer and stare at Alvin and Betsy Cooper. Then a group of girls took him and seated him on one of the canopied thrones, while another group, boys, took Betsy Cooper and seated her on the other throne, facing him across the hall. Again the drum rolled, Miss Waite spoke, and the girls placed a leafy crown on Alvin's head, while the boys placed a similar crown on Betsy Cooper's head. Then everyone applauded and backed away, leaving an open aisle between the thrones.

When the music started again, it was a song Alvin recognized,

"Earth Angel," and he began to hum along. He looked up and saw that Betsy Cooper had left her throne and was walking steadily, slowly towards him. He met her halfway across the room, and, as soon as they started to dance together, all the other people paired off and danced with them.

At the end of the song, Alvin dropped Betsy Cooper's hand as if it were a snake, and cut through the laughing crowd for the door. He found his coat on a chair beside the door, put it on, and rushed outside. He was feeling light now, almost as if he were filled with air, and very warm, and he ran in long, bouncing strides, leaps practically, across the parking lot, between the rows of cars towards the far, dark corner of the lot, where Feeney had parked.

But when he reached the corner, it was empty. Feeney and Bilodeau had gone. He stood for a second in the spot where the car had been, between two pickup trucks. Turning to leave, he heard a voice say mildly, "Alvin, wait. Wait."

He spun around and saw the figure of a man facing him. It may not have been a man, Alvin couldn't tell for sure, but it was a man-sized person, much taller, in fact, than Alvin himself. The person had blonde hair, very long and worn loosely over his shoulders, like a religious fanatic. He was dressed in a white robe that glistened in the blocks of light that came from the school and streetlights nearby. In one hand he was holding a staff, in the other a fish about the size of a three-pound bass. Alvin noticed that the person was standing on the cold asphalt pavement in his bare feet.

"Are you all right? Alvin asked solicitously.

"Yes, thank you," the person answered. He was extremely handsome, almost beautiful, in a way Alvin had never seen before. His face combined qualities Alvin had never imagined in combination—strength brought together with precision, alongside gentleness and affection, intelligence conjoined to guilelessness, force driven by compassion. Then Alvin saw that the person had wings, large, heavy-feathered, white wings, the tops of which arched a little ways above his shoulders before falling away almost to the ground.

"Should I know you?" Alvin asked the angel.

"No, probably not."

"Who are you, then?"

"I'm Raphael, one of the Seven."

"Oh?"

"Yes, the healer," he explained, smiling sympathetically at the boy. Turning slowly, his body began to lift off the ground, like a dirigible, and then his wings started flapping, and he flew heavily up from the parking lot and headed west, towards the center of town, where he disappeared over the Union Building.

When the angel was finally gone from sight, Alvin walked slowly away, leaving the parking lot for the road. He figured that if he walked right along, he'd have no trouble getting home before midnight.

He was right, and as soon as he got home, he told his mother, who was up waiting for him, that he had decided to become a minister, and in the morning he told his father the same thing. His mother seemed happier with his decision than his father did, but that was mainly because his father didn't really believe he meant it. Naturally, he told neither of them what had been his alternative to the ministry. Nor did he say anything to them about the angel.

II

Chub Feeney introduced them. Alvin was in the driver's seat of his own car, his beefy arm dangling like a sleeping gorilla's from the open window. He took a long look at the girl as she and Feeney walked out of the roller-skating rink and crossed the parking lot, and he thought, Oh, God, she's not a *girl,* she's a *grown woman!*

Feeney laid one skinny hand on the roof of Alvin's new car—his own, light blue, ten-year-old Ford sedan that he had sold to Alvin for two hundred dollars three weeks ago—and with his other hand exhibited the girl to his friend, as if she were a quarterhorse and Alvin a prospective buyer. "There ya go, Al. This here's Miss Mary Buck."

Alvin nodded glumly, more to Feeney than to Miss Buck.

"This here's my friend, Al. Al Stock. Al's studyin' to be a minister, y' see, so I knew you wouldn't mind ridin' in front with him," he said, grinning at her.

"No, I don't mind a bit. How d'yer do," she said somberly in a clipped accent. She was about twenty-four or -five, and large, muscular, with big breasts, shoulders, and arms. Her face was plain but not unattractive, slightly freckled, big-boned, with a large, loose mouth and pushy chin. She wore her dark hair short, close to the skull, and was dressed in tight black-and-white vertical-striped Bermuda shorts and a crisp white short-sleeved blouse. Though she was in every way clean looking, like a cake of soap, she didn't look at all naive or innocent to Alvin. Walking swiftly around the front of the car, she swung open the door and immediately slid over beside him on the seat.

Feeney got in the back and lit a cigarette.

"Got a fag?" Mary Buck asked.

"A what?" Feeney asked her.

"A cigarette. Can I have one?"

"Oh, yeah, yeah, sure." He handed her the pack, and she took out four or five and passed the pack back.

The car was parked at the end of the lot in the front row, facing the lake, which was narrow here where it closed to form Alton Bay. On the other side of the water, Alvin could see the headlights of cars heading north from the bay towards Wolfeboro. "Where to?" he asked Feeney.

"The Dockside, that restaurant back in the town a ways. We're picking up sister Ruth there. She's an old friend of mine," Feeney said.

"She gets off work in fifteen minutes," Mary Buck added.

"You Canadian?" Alvin asked her. He wondered about her name. What kind of a name was Buck?

"Yup. Nova Scotian." She pronounced it "Novi Skolshun." She'd come down from her hometown to the States for the summer to work at one of the restaurants and share a cottage on the lake with her younger sister Ruth. Her sister was going back at the end of the month, had to be home for school by Labor Day, but she planned on going on down to Boston to look for a job there. She was tired of life in Canada. "It's a boring place," she said flatly. "Boring."

"Yeah," Feeney said. "Let's go, Parson. I got a date."

"Are you really studyin' to be a preacher?" Mary Buck asked him.

Alvin started the motor, put it in reverse, and backed the slope-shouldered vehicle away from the curbing. "Feeney's a great kidder," he answered. It was too hard to explain. He wished he'd never mentioned it to Feeney, or anyone else, for that matter. Although he was glad he had told Betsy Cooper. A few people seemed to understand, or at least to respect his decision to enter the ministry. Especially Betsy Cooper. "Wow, that's really neat," she had said one night in May, after a meeting of the French Club. He and Betsy had been standing outside the school under a streetlight, waiting for Feeney to pick them up, as he had promised, and drive Betsy home for Alvin. Betsy Cooper was now understood to be Alvin's girlfriend, but without a car of his own, the best he could offer her, whenever possible, was the service of his friend Feeney's car, which his friend Feeney grudgingly permitted.

"Yes," he had told her. "I've decided to go into the ministry. I think it's important for a man to choose a career that will allow him to help other people, don't you?"

"Oh, yes, sure. Did you think about becoming a doctor? You're awfully good in math and science and stuff like that, you know."

"I thought about it, yes. But I'm not cut out for it. Money just doesn't mean that much to me."

"I know."

"I want to be able to help people, maybe as a missionary. Maybe work in Africa or India or Chicago or someplace like that, working to give people a chance to do something constructive with their lives."

"My dad wanted to be a minister once. Then he went into business. But I really respect you for it. It's not an easy life. Especially if you become a missionary."

"I know."

"I never knew you were . . . religious, though. I mean, you never seemed . . . that way," she had said.

"Well, I guess in the usual way I'm really not very religious, not in the usual way. I'm not one of your Bible-thumping church-goers, who I regard as mostly hypocrites anyway. I've been reading theology a lot. When I decide what church I think is right, you know, about religion, then I'll go to that church and I'll support it right down the line. I'll put my life on the line for it. But until I can find a church I can put my life on the line for, I'm not going to run around shouting Hallelujah, praise the Lord, all that sort of thing, you know. It's an inner experience, religion. It's not something you can join, like the Elks or the Republican Party," he had told her. "It's an inner experience, private. Which you can later translate into action. In society."

"I really respect that," she had said, her nostrils flaring.

Ruth Buck, Mary Buck's little sister, was already waiting for them when they arrived outside the darkened restaurant. Alvin let his car coast to a silent stop beside her. Shorter and heavier than her older sister, she was also, in a conventional way, prettier—her features were not so pronounced, and she thus could be described as "cute," which could hardly be said of Mary Buck.

"How old're you?" Mary Buck asked him. Her sister was climbing into the back seat next to Feeney.

"Uh . . . sixteen." No sense in lying. Feeney knew the truth anyhow. He would have liked to have said nineteen, though.

"Not old enough."

"Huh?"

"I'll buy the beer. We can stop at a little store a ways up the road. You two got some money?" she asked the boys.

Feeney handed a couple of dollars over the seat. "That there's my friend Al. Al, this here's Ruth. She's in love with me. Ain't you, honey?" He started to nuzzle the girl along the back of her neck, and she giggled. She was wearing a waitress's uniform and over it a tan trench coat. Somehow girls with trench coats were sexy to Alvin. He half-expected every girl with a trench coat to have nothing on underneath it.

"How about you?" Mary Buck asked him. She pronounced it "a-boot."

"What?"

"The money. For the beer."

"Oh, yeah, sure." He took two dollars from his wallet, the only bills in there, and gave them to her. "That enough?" he inquired casually.

"Yeah. I'll get quarts."

In the rear-view mirror Alvin could see Feeney and Ruth Buck squirming against one another. Feeney's hands were plunging deep into the girl's trench coat. "Jesus," Alvin thought.

"Let's go," Mary Buck said impatiently. "We can stop at that little grocery store up the road and I'll run in and get the beer. Our place is a couple of miles beyond it, towards Wolfeboro. We can go there," she informed him.

"Okay," Alvin said, turning the car around, heading it north along the bay, hoping as he drove that he had enough gas in the car to make it to wherever they were going and back home to Crawford again, because he was out of money now, and he couldn't imagine himself asking Feeney for any, especially in front of Mary Buck. The two dollars he had given her were actually his last two dollars in the world, with no more money immediately forthcoming. A week ago he had quit working part-time for his father by announcing to him that this summer he was planning to work on the staff of a Presbyterian boys' camp on Lake Winnipesaukee. The announcement had been a difficult one for him to make—he knew what his father's assumptions were, what they had been all year. Very carefully, as tactfully as he knew how, he had explained to his father that this summer, because of his long-range plans, he thought it would be better for him if he took a job that brought him into contact with what he called "Christian Work." And he knew of a boys' camp, Camp Leelanau, run by the Presbyterian Church, that was looking for summer help.

"As what?"

He wasn't sure. General staff, he supposed. Maybe just kitchen help or maintenance or something. The counselors were all college boys studying to become ministers, so he knew they wouldn't want him to be a counselor, not yet. A dishwasher, maybe.

"Jee-sus," his father snorted. "Boy, this minister thing of yours is the goddamnedest idea you've *ever* come up with! You *know* it ain't gonna last, don't you?"

"No. Why shouldn't it last? You wanted to become a plumber,
and that lasted."

His father snorted again and laughed, once, vacantly. "Hah!
Wanted to become a goddamned plumber! Who *ever* wanted to
become a plumber?"

"What *did* you want to be, then?"

"Nothin'. At least I never wanted to become a fuckin' *minister,*"
he sneered, throwing his tools into the bed of the pickup. "Oh, sure,
it might've occurred to me, if I'd ever met a minister I liked. But I
never did, not once. And you never have either, I'll bet. And that's
how come I know this thing'll never last," he declared, as he got into
the truck and closed the door beside him with a rattling slam. He
jammed a cigarette into his mouth, clenching it with his lips, lit it,
and started the motor of the truck. "Well, you just go right ahead,
boy, and you spend your summer washin' dishes for the Lord, but
don't forget, when you get tired of that, you're still going to need a
job so you can afford to drive your girlfriends around in that fancy
new car of yours. Not to mention fifteen bucks a week room and
board here. And I'm not holding this job open for you. No, sir.
There's lots of other kids around town who'll be damned happy laying soilpipe this summer for a buck-fifty an hour." Then he popped
the clutch and drove out of the barn, considerably faster than usual.

That bastard, Alvin thought when his father had cleared the
driveway and disappeared down the road. All he ever paid me was a
buck twenty-five an hour. And I know that's all he planned to pay
me this summer, too.

Mary Buck signaled that the grocery store was just around the
next bend, and Alvin obediently rounded the bend, pulled off the
road, and came to a stop in front of the dark, asphalt-shingled
country store. They waited in the car with the motor running while
Mary Buck went inside the store, and as soon as she returned, lug-
ging two large bags filled with quarts of beer, and got in, Alvin spun
out of the gravel lot and, as the car hit the asphalt, squealed his tires.
Nobody said a word to acknowledge the noise, but, for Alvin, the
group's sudden, brief silence was sufficiently complimentary to his

vehicle and him that his fluttering stomach settled down and all the watery feelings about his diminished worth evaporated completely. He drove along the winding, narrow road like an athlete, letting his body on its own take care of how he got from one place on the road to another, his mind rapt and admiring from afar. The top-heavy old Ford floated and leaned around the corners, and the four passengers drifted smoothly, pleasantly, from side to side with each swing out and back.

After a few minutes Mary Buck said to him, "Left turn at the row of mailboxes up there," and when Alvin saw the mailboxes posted at the side of the road like sentries, he turned onto a trail leading gradually downhill through pines towards the lake, with small cottages scattered among the trees. Most of the cottages were occupied, with cars wearing Massachusetts and Connecticut number plates parked outside, and inside, orange lights on in the kitchens and living rooms.

He was driving very slowly now—because the road was so twisted and narrow and the bumps in it were spring-breakers—and as the car neared the lake, he could hear the chirp and creak of crickets and frogs and, in the pines, the cool night wind off the water. When they came out from under the dark trees where the road reached the shore and stopped against a railroad-tie curbing, the sky seemed suddenly to lift and brighten. In the southeast the moon was nearly full, hanging white and swollen above them, in silver pieces on the water below them. They got out of the car and for a second stood between the two images on a smooth, fragrant carpet of pine needles, when Mary Buck ordered Alvin and Feeney to hurry up and grab the beer and follow her.

She led them through puddles of moonlight along a gravel walkway to a cottage surrounded by tall pines. The cottage was small, little more than a pair of attached overnight cabins with adjoining front porches. One room was used as a combination kitchen and living room, the other was the bedroom. A tiny bathroom was fastened onto the back of the building, like an appendage. The place was sparsely furnished with chairs, a table, a couch, a pair of beds, and a dresser, all of which appeared to have been salvaged at the last possible moment from a condemned boardinghouse.

Alvin took a look around the place and, flopping onto the couch, decided that he loved it. He didn't know why, with its shabbiness and clutter and even filth, but the place delighted him. He grinned and thought: This place could be *anywhere* —California, or Michigan, or Canada, or Mexico—anywhere!

Feeney and Ruth Buck headed straight for the bedroom, and Mary Buck went to work, cracking open two bottles of beer, pulling down the tattered window shades, setting a stack of 45's onto the portable record player and turning the machine on, one by one switching off the orange lights in the room—until in darkness she was sitting next to Alvin on the couch, her arms thrown around his neck, her wet mouth all over his, her breasts shoving his shirtfront, and he suddenly found himself going down backwards beneath her in the noisy, whirling darkness of the room, helpless against the force of Mary Buck's gnashing mouth.

After what seemed like an hour to him, he hollered for Feeney. "Hey, man! We gotta get back! Let's go, lover!"

A few minutes later Feeney appeared at the bedroom door, naked, a thin stripe of moonlight crossing his bony white chest. He whined a bit, standing first on one leg, then on the other, but finally, sourly, agreed. "It's your car. Next time we'll take my ol' man's car," he added grumpily, and disappeared into the bedroom.

Back on the road, passing quickly through Alton Bay south towards Crawford, Feeney finally relented and started talking to his friend again. "Oh, wow, man, didja dork her, man? Did ya screw her to the wall? She's got a big pair of tits. D'ja dork 'er?"

"Oh yeah," Alvin said smoothly.

"Wow! Fuckin'-A, man! Way t' go, man! Y' lost your cherry! The fuckin' parson lost his cherry! Hey—whadda fuckin' pair a tits, that's what I call knockers."

"Yeah. Melons."

"Melons. Yeah, melons all right. You got it made now, Parson," Feeney informed him. "You know that? Made in the shade."

"What do you mean?"

"That job at the camp, man. You lucky bastard. You're gonna be up here all summer, working right down the road from that fuckin' broad. You can knock off a piece of ass any goddamn time you feel like it! Rip off a piece before breakfast, if you want!" Feeney said enviously. "Oh, you got it fuckin'-A made in the shade."

"Yeah," Alvin said, his mind switching frantically back to the interview, that same afternoon, with the director of the camp, a young Presbyterian minister from Newton, Massachusetts. When Alvin had stumbled over "Reverend MacLarendon," the young man had said, "Call me Bruce, okay?" Bruce was sweating grey blossoms through his white Camp Leelanau T-shirt as he talked, still somewhat out of breath after a strenuous tennis match with the redheaded, ample-breasted, middle-aged dietician, who had smiled fetchingly at Alvin as she walked by them on her way to her cabin. "Drinks before dinner, Bruce?" she had called to the sandy-haired man.

"Fine," he had answered, and then had gone back to interviewing Alvin for the dishwasher's job. "That's Joanie Williams, Al. The dietician. Great gal, everyone at Leelanau adores her. We're kind of a family here, Al, you can probably feel that in the air. It's an essential part of the place, the way it works. 'The Leelanau Experience' is something everyone shares in, Al, something that's created and experienced by every single person at Leelanau, whether he's a first-year camper, a member of the staff, a counselor, one of the maintenance people, or part of the administration—everyone, regardless of his or her station here. 'The Leelanau Experience,' Al, it's good cheer, healthy competitiveness, spiritual questing, and affectionate, mutual respect. Plus something intangible, Al, something that none of us can define, especially to someone like yourself, Al, who hasn't experienced it yet."

It all seemed a bit strange to Alvin, somehow too explicitly sincere, with too little mutual fear and mistrust for him not to fear and mistrust it a little and not to fall into a certain insincerity himself. "Sounds *great* to me!" he had exclaimed. Then he had asked about the pay, and for an answer had been shown the spotless cabin used by the kitchen help. Well, he thought, at least I won't have to pay out fifteen a week room and board to my father.

"One day a week off—which day depends on the lots drawn by the rest of the crew—and two hundred dollars a month. Of course, you eat pretty well here at Leelanau, Al. Every kitchen crew we've had so far has ended up with a weight problem by the end of the summer," Bruce had joked.

Alvin laughed uproariously.

"So what do you say, friend? The campers'll start marching in on Monday. We'll need you then."

Alvin had agreed to accept the job, had agreed with outspoken enthusiasm and endless gratitude.

But the second he had departed from the campgrounds, had put the low wood-frame cabins and playing fields, the boathouses and docks, the Main Hall, the Chapel in the Pines, the arts and crafts building, the buzzing lawnmowers and puck-puck sounds of tennis balls batting back and forth, and Bruce, good old Bruce, behind him, and had started back down the road to Alton Bay to pick up Feeney at the Dockside, where an hour earlier he'd left him talking over the counter to the waitress, he suddenly had buckled under the weight of deep misgivings and waves of unexplainable depression. Driving his car into the Dockside parking lot, he had decided not to take the job. He promised himself that he'd call Bruce from the Dockside and tell him he'd made a mistake, his father was going to need him this summer after all.

Which promise he quickly kept, and consequently, from the moment of hanging the phone back on the hook, he'd put the whole thing out of his mind, had refused to think about the camp or the job at all for the remainder of the afternoon and evening—until now, driving home with Feeney, when he could no longer avoid it.

"You got it fuckin'-A made, man, with that job at the camp," Feeney said again. He lit a cigarette and flipped the match neatly into the woods flashing past them.

Alvin thought, Everyone wants me to take the job at the camp. Even Pa, who needs to prove a point by it but can't admit it to himself. And Ma had thought it was a good idea, he reminded himself.

"It'll give you the chance to associate with a better class of people," she had said to him. Miss Waite, his English teacher, had been the one to tell him about the job at Leelanau in the first place. "I'd like to recommend you for the position, Alvin. I think it would be a valuable experience for you." He had known what she meant: that the job would give him a chance to associate with a better class of people than his parents. Essentially the same thing his mother had meant. He had asked Mr. Plumley, his math teacher and football coach, to be his second character reference, and Mr. Plumley had told him, "Al, there's not another man in this school I'd rather recommend for a job like that. As far as I'm concerned, and I'll tell them this, you're the best math student and the best right guard I've ever had the good fortune to work with in my seventeen years at Pittsfield High. You're going far, Al, if you can get a few breaks, and I'll be happy to do what I can to help make those breaks. For once, I'll be running interference for *you.*"

Alvin knew that Coach Plumley, like Miss Waite and his mother, disapproved of his continuing to work for his father. He supposed they were afraid that he would end up like his father—a plumber. Even for Betsy Cooper it was the same fear. For her as much as for the rest of them, and maybe even for his father, too, anything that seemed to draw the arc of his future away from his father's present was to be encouraged, even if it meant, with his working at the camp, they would not see as much of him in the summer months. And even if, superficially at least, his taking that job contributed to his projected life in the ministry. He would call Bruce again in the morning, first thing. He figured Bruce was an early riser. He'd just tell him that he'd made a mistake, his father didn't really need him after all.

He turned off the main road and drove slowly through Crawford Center. He realized that he and Feeney hadn't said a word to each other since Alton Bay. Amazing, he thought, how suddenly everything can go quiet without your even knowing it. He dropped Feeney off in front of his house, and then drove home.

Part II: Transformation

"Jesus!" I said. "Is there a new world here?" "Of course," said he. "But it isn't in the least new. They do say, indeed, that outside there is a new earth, where they have both Sun and Moon, and that it's packed full of fine things. But this one here is the older."

—Rabelais, *Gargantua and Pantagruel,* Book II, ch. 32

The Rise of the Middle Class

Weary, half-defeated by history and almost as wary of those you have spent your life's energies and treasure to make free as you are of their iron-minded oppressors, you are the middle-aging Simón Bolívar, and less than a month ago you arrived here in Kingston in desperate flight from Venezuela, arrived with a Spanish price on your head and a pack of rabid assassins dogging your trail down from the mountains of Colombia to the sea, always hoping you would stupidly trust someone you should not. You did not, and, happily, the assassins seem not to have followed you here, at least not yet.

It is the afternoon of the seventh of June, 1815. Your friend, Mr. Henry Cullen, has invited you to leave Kingston and visit with him at his plantation in Falmouth, a Great House situated on a limestone cliff overlooking Jamaica's tranquil north shore, and you have gratefully accepted. The effort of trying to convince agents of the English king to support you and your ragtag rebellions against the Spanish king has angered and exhausted you. And neither anger nor exhaustion becomes you. Your pale, delicate face and frame, your intelligence, your exquisitely refined (yet passionate) sensibility, these become clouded and only vaguely felt, by you or anyone else, when you are angry; and when you are exhausted, you fear that you resemble an aesthete, a type of human being you abhor.

"Yes, my dear friend," you write to Cullen, scratch-scratch against the parchment. "I shall arrive one week from tomorrow, probably rather late in the day, for your Jamaican roadways are not much smoother or straighter than my beloved Venezuelan mountain paths."

You put down the pen, and the first of the assassins to reach the island, one López Martínez Martínez, springs through the open door from the balcony outside, grabs you by the ruffled collar of your shirt, and raises his knife. His eyes are reddened with lust for the paid killing, and, you note absurdly, he smells of goat cheese and wet canvas. He is grinning wildly, his red tongue afloat in his toothless mouth.

When your shirt tears in his grip, you yank yourself away from him as if he were a disease, knocking over the escritoire, and your letter to Cullen falls to the parquet floor like a leaf, slips onto the balcony and off, drifting whitely to the sunny courtyard below, where it is seen by a black man, an English slave named Jack, commonly called Three-Fingered Jack, for he has lost two fingers on his right hand. He squints and stares up, as if to see where the paper might have come from. He could, if he wished, peer across the balcony outside your room through the open doors into your room and watch you struggle with the assassin.

Jack says nothing. He walks slowly over and casually picks up your unfinished letter to Cullen, folds it carefully in half and half again, and slides it between his sweaty belly and leather belt. Surely Jack does not worry about your welfare. He must know that you are an important man, that you have two British soldiers from Fort Charles posted outside your door, and that they will hear your struggle with Martínez Martínez and will save you. Jack doubtless wants your piece of paper. Paper is useful and not cheap.

Later in the day, you look around your room for your letter to Cullen. You search under the bed and the dresser, even inside the mahogany wardrobe. It's nowhere to be seen. Where could it have flown to? Curious.

Finally, you sit down at the escritoire and begin again, even more wearily and gratefully than when you wrote the first letter. "My dear Henry, your kind offer to remove me from the swelter and the crowds of Kingston to the refreshing luxury of your Great House has been received here with delight and great relief, for I was beginning to believe that I . . ."

When you have completed the letter and have sealed it with wax, you rise from the table, go to the door of your chamber, and hand the letter to the guard outside, instructing him to post it immediately to Falmouth. Then, feeling both enervated and oddly agitated—because of Martínez Martínez, you tell yourself, in spite of the fact that he is now quite dead, a chunk of meat with a mouth shuddering with flies—you walk to the balcony and peer down into the courtyard.

The packed earth is cream colored from the sun. A black man works alone down there, raking away the tracks of the horses, smoothing the grounds, pulling slowly on his split-bamboo rake, moving the riffles and ripples in the dirt, the clods kicked loose by the horses' hooves, the droppings, and the leaf or stalk that may have idly fallen to the ground after having been blown into the court-yard from beyond the walls by an errant puff of wind off the bay. Slowly, tediously, he pulls these tiny disturbances in gradually closing concentric circles. From above, you examine the circles closely, and eventually you realize that they are spirals, coils, moving towards a still center which, with a wide, square-bladed shovel, the black man will remove and deposit outside the gate. The design will be gone. Without the center, there will be no spiral, no coil.

You study the man for a moment. He is a slave. A man wholly inside history, you reflect. No one will assassinate him. He can only be murdered. To be assassinated, you must first step outside history; you have to be guilty of trying to affect history from outside. Like God. But the slave, by definition, can never obtain that prerogative, you observe. You envy him. More and more often, in recent months, you have found yourself envying people you regard as being wholly determined by the sweep of history. The shepherd in Peru. The Inca baby outside the cathedral in Bogotá. The sailor on the British frigate that brought you to Kingston. And now this one, a slave.

You think: That man probably has my letter to Cullen, the first one. He probably saw it skitter out the open door to the balcony, the very door that the assassin entered. He probably saw the assassin climb the tile drain to the narrow ledge and watched him crawl along the ledge to the balcony, saw him swing his legs over the balcony rail, open the door an inch wider and stroll into my room, the knife already in his hand.

But even so, you bear the slave no malice. Quite the contrary. No, to be free to stand there below and watch one man attempt to assassinate another, and to be able to do nothing—what a respite! You sigh. Then you squint and look closely, and you realize that the black man has seen you staring down at him. He is staring back. He probably envies me, you think. What an irony, you smile. To envy the man who envies you.

It is late. The sun drifts closer to the horizon above the bay and the flatlands to the west of Kingston. Beyond the fortress walls lies the turquoise sea, now smeared red by the setting sun, as if with blood. You are growing morose, so you "pull yourself together," as the English say, and in your mind compose the first sentence of yet another letter to the editors of the Kingston newspapers, *The Royal Gazette* and *The St. Jago Gazette*. Here is the sentence: "Sir: To the everlasting credit and glory of His Royal Majesty King George III and the Royal Governor of Jamaica, the Duke of Manchester, it is true that today the lowliest blackamoor in this paradise, a three-fingered negro slave named Jack, is more to be envied than the founder of a Republic torn from the darkly bleeding heart of the mighty South American continent."

You believe that the English will believe that this is true; you know that at this moment, for you, it is true; and you also know that Three-Fingered Jack, if he could read your letter, would laugh. But the obligation to shape a future history forbids that you say what is true for everyone. Such a freedom would allow only that you doodle and dribble, that you waste time and paper while you sit here in a fortress by the sea, helplessly waiting for the Spanish Empire to crack at its feeble feet and drop its heavy head down parapets, cliffs, palisadoes, campaniles. You think of equestrian statues toppling from building-sized bases. You think of armored Arab horses stumbling on the pampas and shattering their thin, brittle legs. You think of cashew trees sprawling heavily across spindly trunks. You think of a waterspout. "If only," you murmur, and the images of collapse multiply.

It is dark. The room is filled with maroon and purple wedges of shadow. Again you stroll to the balcony and look into the courtyard. Down there it is now wholly dark. You can see nothing definite. A pit of blackness. Noise of leather moving against leather, of horses breathing, of a man's callused hand moving across his forearm against the hairs—these carefully rise through the silence to you.

He's still down there. You know he's down there, buried in the darkness the same way he's buried in history. As if to extend the metaphor and thus complete the communiqué, you light the lantern behind you and place it on the escritoire. You step in front of it to the edge of the balcony. You show yourself in sharp profile. A shot rings out.

Indisposed

Lie in bed. Just lie there. Don't move, stare at the ceiling and don't blink. Keep your fingers from twitching. Let your weight press into the mattress. Take shallow, slow breaths, so that the covers neither rise nor fall. Feel the heavy, inert length of your body. The whole of it, from your head to your feet, like the trunk of a fallen tree moldering and sinking slowly into the damp soft ground of the forest.

For that is how he likes you best—your husband William. You are Jane Hogarth, wife to the painter, keeper of his house and bed. He sees you as a great tall tree that he is too short to climb, except when you are prone, cut down by the ax of his temper, or drawn down by his words, his incessant words, the need that drives them.

It's now mid-morning. You are indisposed and have remained here in bed, as if it were a choice, a decision not to rise at dawn, empty the pots, wash and dress, brush out your hair, descend the stairs to the kitchen, build the fire and start preparing the day's food, send Ellen to the market, organize the wash, beat the carpets, sweep and wash the floors, the two of you—the big, slow-moving, careful woman and her helper, that skinny, nervous, rabbit-like girl Ellen.

You're a poor combination, you and that girl. Together you seem to break more crockery, waste more time, do more work than either of you would do alone. You follow each other around as if setting right what the other must have done wrong. You never should have agreed to take her in, but she is your cousin, a Thornhill, and her family could not hold her at home in the country any longer. It was the only way to keep the girl from becoming a harlot. William insisted on it. Absolutely insisted.

Of course he insisted, you reflect. They're just alike, he and that tiny quick girl. They probably have the same appetites. If he did not have this house and you to run it, to keep it clean and comfortable and filled with food and drink for him and his friends, he would have long ago died a rake's miserable death. And he knows it. He saw that girl and recognized the temperament and he knew the way she would go if you did not take her in. He sat there in his short-legged chair in the corner, the only chair in the house that lets his feet rest flatly on the floor, and his eyes and hands and mouth would not stop moving until you relented.

We can't set her onto the streets, and your uncle won't let her return home, and her mind seems set on the city life, and on and on he chattered, while his hands moved jerkily across the paper on his lapboard, and his eyes jumped like blue fleas, and the girl wrung her hands and spun around, dropping her bonnet, stooping to retrieve it, knocking over the water pitcher and basin on the table next to her, all the while apologizing and blathering as much family gossip into your face as she could think of, probably making most of it up, just to keep on reminding you that you too are a Thornhill and that she is the daughter of your famous father's country brother.

Maybe my father—, you tried to say, but he wouldn't let you finish. No, no, no, no, he said, his eyes still hopping over the girl, leaping from her clear face to her fresh young bosom to her slender hips and back again, as she spun and wrung and bumped into things. No, your father's house is already too crowded. All those apprentices, maids, all those children, patrons, hangers-on. And how many cousins already in from the country. Even he himself, your father, couldn't say. No, our house is quite large enough, she should stay here with us. After all, there's only the two of us . . . and you need a helper, he said, suddenly turning his gaze on you, as if you had just entered the room.

His eyes filled wetly with sympathy for you. You nodded your head slowly up and down, and his eyes went swiftly back to the girl, his

hands back to the drawing on his lap. Then, the matter settled and
the drawing finished, he stopped, folded the sheet of paper in half,
stood up and went out the door to the street, calling over his shoulder as he rounded the corner that he wouldn't be back till later this
evening.

Which you knew. No reason for him even to say that much anymore. He'll come home sometime after midnight, smelling of wine
and beef fat and whores, humming downstairs in the kitchen as he
rummages for a piece of cake or a slice of cold meat. Then he'll
bump his way up the stairs, and he'll be on you, climbing up and
over you with his nervous little body, already stiff and pressing
against you with it, prodding, poking, groping, his hands yanking at
your breasts, his wet mouth jammed against your dry throat, until
finally, to stop him from jabbing himself against you, you spread
your large thighs and let him enter you, and for a few moments, as if
searching for your womb, he leaps around inside you.

Then, at last, he sighs and releases his grip on your breasts and
slides out of you and off. You hear him standing in the darkness
buttoning himself up. He wobbles unsteadily from the room and
down the hallway to his own room. A few minutes pass in silence,
and he begins to snore. And you lie in your bed and stare blankly
into the sea of darkness that surrounds you.

Now, this morning, when Ellen comes to your door and asks what
should she do today, you say that you are indisposed, meaning that
you cannot come down today—as if it were a choice, a decision. You
almost remind the rabbit-like girl that after three months in the
house she should know what to do. You remember that you yourself
knew after three months what was expected. And you had no patient,
calm, competent older woman to teach you the intricacies of house-
keeping. Ellen walks off with her chamber pot in hand, and you lie
there in your bed, preferring to have the girl think you have decided
to stay in bed today, like a lady of leisure, than that she know the
truth.

For the truth is that you have made no decision at all. Not to rise,
and not to stay abed. When you woke at dawn, it was as if you had
not wakened at all. You had merely slipped from sleep into a world

where neither sleep nor wakefulness existed, where you could neither act nor not act. And so you lie here, hoping that by imitating a corpse you will at least seem to be in the same world as the people around you. They will think you are present, even if only as a corpse. But you are not present. You are absent, gone from this house, its clutter of beds, pots, chairs, tables, bottles, linens, carpets, dogs, and clothes, and gone from the people who live here, that taut young woman downstairs in the kitchen and the man who went out to his studio early this morning, as always, that man, that chattering, growling, barking, little man, his bristling red hair and bright little eyes, his jerky hands and his sudden switches of mood, words, movement, direction. You are absent from them both. Gone. Your body remains behind you, like your clothes and hairbrush. Your large, strong, smooth-moving body. Your barren body.

And so, helpless, you lie in bed. You can't move. You stare at the ceiling and you cannot blink your eyes, even as the shadows fade and the afternoon light scours the plaster to a white glare. You feel your weight press steadily into the mattress. You take shallow, slow breaths, and the covers neither rise nor fall. You feel the heavy, inert length of your long body, from the crown of your head to the soles of your feet, as if it were the trunk of a fallen tree moldering and sinking slowly into the damp soft ground of the forest.

Suddenly he is in the room, standing next to the bed. Your husband, William Hogarth, the famous painter and engraver. You stare at the ceiling but you know he is standing there beside you. You can hear his quick, gulping breaths, can smell his sweat and his mouth, the kidney pie and ale he had for lunch. He is asking questions, making demands for answers. His voice barks at you. Then, leaning over you, blocking your view of the ceiling, he stares into your eyes, and his expression changes from that of an annoyed man to that of a wondering man. But he is not happy when he is a wondering man, and his expression swiftly changes back to one of annoyance.

It occurs to you that he will beat you again, will double those hard small fists of his and throw them at you, as if you were in a pit and he were stoning you from above. You are not afraid. Not now. Not anymore. You are absent now, and though he may bury you in this pit with his stony fists, he will bury only your barren body, as if he were pummeling a pile of some poor woman's old clothes.

Then, as suddenly as he came, he is gone. You are alone again. The shadows on the ceiling, long grey wedges, have returned. Falling—, you are falling and flying away at the same time, from this thick body, from the bed, its four carved posts, from the room itself, the clutter, the babble of furniture, crockery, clothes, and carpets, even away from the house, and the crowd standing wide eyed on the narrow street in front, gaping skyward as you fly and fall away from them. It's what he would want. You are pleasing him at last. You have left behind what he wants—your large, slow body, your silence, and your acceptance of his blows, his words, his pushing, stiff little body, his seed. You are pleasing him at last.

You watch him return to the house with the doctor in tow. They are both out of breath and red faced as they come through the door and enter the bedroom. It is dusk. The doctor asks for light, and in a few seconds Ellen appears next to them with a lit candle. The doctor, a short man, almost as short as your husband, but older, rounder, dirtier, takes the candle from the girl and holds it near your face. You watch them all—the somber, wheezing doctor with the stained fingers, the fair-haired, pink-faced girl, her new breasts popping above her bodice like fresh pears, and your husband, bobbing nervously behind, talking, talking, making suggestions, asking quick questions, recalling similar cases. From time to time he looks at the girl's breasts and goes silent.

You watch them all, including the one they are examining, the body on the bed. It is the largest body in the room, the strongest, the only healthy body in the room. The doctor's lungs are bad, his face is red and blotched with purple islands and broken veins, and his hands are stunted and bent from arthritis. The girl, though young, is nervous and cannot eat without suffering great stomach pain. Her blonde hair has started to fall out in thatches when she brushes it in the morning. And your husband, when he rises, coughs bits of blood, suffers from excruciating headaches, and has had three attacks of gout in this one year. Your body, though, lying there below you, is an athlete's, unblemished, bulky, powerful, and smooth. That's what

they're trying to save, that's what they believe they can save—your
big, healthy body. They need it, and it lies on its back, like a wagon
without wheels. They are all annoyed. Why won't it work? they ask
each other. What's wrong with this big, strong, in all observable
ways healthy body?

The doctor asks the girl what were the exact words your body
uttered this morning when she came to the room to check on it, to
see why it was not performing its usual tasks.

Indisposed. It said it was indisposed, the girl tells the man.
Nothing more. No complaints or anything. The girl's hands are in
fists jammed against her hips.

The doctor takes a small vial from his case and with one crippled
hook-like hand prods open the mouth of your body. With the other
he empties the vial into it. Then he closes the mouth, massages the
muscular throat, forcing the body to swallow. It swallows the thick,
salty fluid, and the doctor releases the throat, content.

He wipes the mouth of the grey vial with his fingers and places it
neatly into his case. I've given it a purgative, he says to your husband.
By morning it should be back to normal again. You can do without it
till then, can't you? the physician asks him, winking.

Your husband grins and looks at Ellen's breasts. Of course, he
says, and invites the doctor downstairs for a drink and something to
eat. The girl Ellen runs ahead to prepare the table for the men.

Now your body lies alone in the darkening chamber. You watch it
from above, from a place touching the ceiling. The body hears the
doctor laugh, a rumble of voices, chairs against the floor. Then the
sound of the doctor's hearty departure. Laughter of your husband
and Ellen. A door between rooms somewhere downstairs opens and
clicks closed. Carriages pass in the streets, a pair of harlots argues
with a vendor. Someone calls to a departing friend.

The body shudders slowly. A bubble grows inside the belly and
then bursts. The body shudders again, this time more violently. It is
the grey purgative working. Then the body erupts with rumbling
noises from its several orifices, and its surface ripples with muscular
contractions. It is wet with sweat yet goes on shivering as if chilled.
The body continues barking and erupting with noise, sounds of air

under pressure being suddenly released. The sheet is wet, at first with sweat, soaked, but with urine now as well. Then a watery stool trickles from between the buttocks and spreads, foul smelling, beneath the thighs.

The body hears the call of your husband downstairs as he opens the door to the street and informs the girl Ellen that he won't be home till later. Then the sounds of evening drift up the stairs and seep under the closed door of the bedroom—the creaking of the pump, dishes being washed, the sound of cupboard doors being opened and closed, and, after a while, the clicking steps of Ellen past your closed door and up the stairs beyond to her tiny room in the attic. Then silence, except for an occasional passing carriage, a cry from the street, a dog barking.

The body lies motionless in its waters and extrusions, quiet now, the heart beating slowly, regularly, peacefully, the bladder, kidneys, and intestines emptied and at rest, the lungs expanding and contracting with perfect symmetry and ease. For the first time that you can remember, you look down at your large, slow body, and you pity it. For the first time, you pity your body. Until this moment, you have felt either indifference or dislike, annoyance. For it has made you the plain daughter of a famous and demanding father, the one passed over in favor of your smaller, prettier sisters when the young artists and budding courtiers came to call at the home and studio of the grand and official court painter, the newly knighted Sir James Thornhill. It was the body presented at last to that persistent, abrasive one, the tiny man with the grandiose ambitions, almost as a joke, as a way of getting him to go away and cease his incessant talking. Hogarth wants a Thornhill, eh? Well, let him have Jane, let him have the body we call Jane, the cumbersome one, the one that's larger than most men. Let him wake every morning and be reminded of his smallness. Ho, ho, she may turn out to be barren. A good joke on a desperate man, and a solution to the problem posed by a daughter too large and too plain to marry off easily.

You did not pity it then, you were angry with it, annoyed that it should get caught so helplessly in other people's designs for themselves. But you pity it now, tonight, as it lies there below you like a great and dignified beast trapped in quicksand, resigned, yet all its systems functioning efficiently in the darkness, as close to a state of rest as a living organism can come without descending into death. Stasis. You pity it for its very presence in the world, its large and pathetic demands on space, the way it tries and constantly fails to avoid being seen. And the way it has at last given up that attempt, has at last agreed to be seen, to be wholly present. You pity it, and finally you understand it. You understand the body of Jane Hogarth.

From below comes the abrupt noise of your husband returning from the company he keeps, drunkenly bumping furniture and walls as he makes his way in darkness up the narrow stairs. He stops outside your room, where your body lies in its cold juices, pauses for a second, then moves down the hallway. At the attic stairs he stops again. Then slowly he ascends to the attic. His feet scuffle overhead, like rats in the gutter.

Your body slowly stirs, then rises and plucks itself gracefully from the sopped and stinking bed. At the sideboard there is a china pitcher of water and a basin. With a wet cloth and soap, your body slowly washes itself. Delicately, lovingly, the hands move over the shoulders, breasts, and belly, across and between the buttocks and thighs. Even the feet are washed and carefully dried. Then it slips a clean white linen gown on, and, relighting the candle left by Ellen on the sideboard, your body takes its leave of the room, as if the body were a queen leaving her private chambers for court. The body turns left at the door and stops at the bottom of the attic stairs, turns left and mounts the stairs to the attic.

There they are, the man atop the girl in her narrow bed in the corner. They are twined together in a tangle of limbs, blotches of hair, bedclothes in a snarl. You watch as your hands place the candle on a stool by the door and reach across to the man, who, suddenly aware of the presence of your body in the low room, filling it with bulk and swiftness, turns from the girl's shut face and faces yours, as your huge hands grab his shoulders as if they were chunks of mutton and yank him away from the girl's stickily clinging legs. The little man is hefted into the air, and the girl screams. He groans helplessly and is pitched across the room against the wall. Your left hand grabs his throat, lifts him to a standing position, and your right hand, balled into a fist, crashes into his face. Your hand releases his throat and lets his body collapse on the floor, a marionette with its strings cut, where he moans and spits in pain and fear. When your gaze turns back to the girl, the man scuttles like a crab for the door and clatters down the stairs to the hallway below, and, while the girl pleads for her life, he flees through the darkened house for the street, howling through his broken mouth like a dog kicked by a horse. Your right hand slaps the girl powerfully across the side of her small head, then in one continuous motion sweeps through the air to her wicker satchel next to the bed, draws it up and hurls it at her. Her wardrobe is wrenched open and its contents spilled onto the floor, then thrown at the sobbing girl on the bed.

Calmly, with dignity, your tall, broad, powerful body turns and leaves the room, descends the stairs and somberly returns to your bedroom. A new candle is lit, and the bedding is removed and swiftly replaced with clean linen. Then the body slides into the cool, broad bed, covers itself against the chill of the late summer night, and soon falls into an even sleep.

The morning will come, and though many things will still be the same, some things will be different. The girl Ellen will be gone, on the streets of the city or else returned to her father's home in the country. Your husband, his mouth tender for weeks, will be silent but brooding and filled with the resentment that feeds on fear. But he will go on behaving just as before, and in time he will forget this night's fury and your immense power, and his fear will abate, and drunkenly one night he will climb onto your prone body to take his pleasure from it. People will still smile when they see you in the company of your diminutive husband, and it will irritate him, as always, and he will hurriedly walk several paces in front of you. You will remain childless. But never again, for as long as you live, will you be indisposed. You will live in your body as if it were the perfect mate, the adoring father, the admiring handmaiden, the devoted child of your devotions. You will live in your body as if it were your own.

The Caul

You are in Richmond, Virginia, and you can't remember your mother. She was an actress, she was beautiful, they say. No one remembers your father. Of him they say nothing, and so, you believe, it is "natural" that you do not remember him. But your mother carried you here to the city of Richmond—in her arms, in her arms. She languished through the sweltering months of summer. The play moved on to Charleston without her. Her pain increased daily. The coughing from the attic room, the groans, the sudden shrieks. The women muffled your ears against them. You were bad, a bad boy, bad little boy. She died. You can't remember her face, her touch, her smell, her voice, all of which were beautiful, they say. They tell you this even today, the few who knew her those last months. Women, young women then, old women now. You remind them of her. If only *they* could remind *you* of her. You are Edgar Poe the poet, author of "The Raven." In a few moments you will recite that beloved, that "magnificent and profound" poem to the literary citizens of Richmond, Virginia. Afterwards, in the Reverend Doctor Woolsey's parlor, you will describe how you actually composed the poem, the rational procedures by which you constructed it, and they will be amazed. You too will be amazed at this new account of your ingenuity and self-sufficiency, your mastery of the intricacies and logic of language and emotion. And your mother would be amazed too, had she lived to see it, hear it, watch you mystify them by means of demystification, enchant them by means of disenchantment, bewilder them with your clarity. They will feel privileged and released, for you will have demonstrated how any one of them could have written your beloved poem himself, had he merely been willing to apply himself to the task. But you, of course, have been the only one willing to apply himself to the task, and that is the reason the poem is yours, you are its author, you are Edgar Poe the poet. Anyone could be Edgar Poe the poet, anyone, were he merely willing to apply himself to the task. You believe that, and when you politely excuse yourself and depart from the company of these literary ladies and gentlemen of Richmond, Virginia, they will believe it too. It will give them a certain relief. How wonderful, they will each separately think, to know that you could be Edgar Poe the poet if you merely applied yourself to the task. And how wonderful, they will each separately think, to be free not to apply yourself to the task! They will each accept one more glass of sherry, and, in your absence, will admire your elegant yet forceful presence upon the stage, your charm and lucidity in private conversation, your erudition, your "profound and tender" eyes, your "musical" voice, all quite as if each person in the room were separately admiring his own presence upon the stage, his own charm, lucidity, erudition, eyes, voice. They will each separately admire your irresistibly beautiful mind. Your fame. Your position among men. Your role with women. Your exotic past. Your dead mother.

II

You have been seated on a straight-backed chair in the center of the stage. A few feet in front of you, the Reverend Doctor Woolsey reads at the lectern from his prepared introductory speech. You watch his broad back, his speckled hands, his rising fluff of white hair. The thick tube of fat at the base of his skull contracts and hardens, and the Reverend Doctor lifts his gaze to the heavens so as more adequately to praise the poet Edgar Poe author of "The Raven." You. Who cannot remember your mother. In your dreams she appears with her back to you, her arms outstretched before her. She ignores your call of Mother! Mother! It is I, Edgar Poe the poet! But she does not flee or otherwise remove herself from you. She stands there in a white dress, as if at a lectern, with her arms outstretched, her gaze lifted heavenward, as if more adequately to praise her son, or as if to pray for permission for him to join her. For without permission you cannot join her, you may not move your feet, you may not take a single step towards her. It is as if you are bad, a bad boy, bad little boy. That is how she appears in your dreams of her and how you also appear there. A moribund tableau vivant, a frieze cut in a wall of darkness. Not a conscious memory, though. For when, awake, you try to remember your mother, as you do now, you remember nothing, and no mind can picture nothing, and so you remember Mr. Allan and the tobacco warehouses, the canal alongside the James River, your cousin Virginia and her mother. You recall your room at the college in Charlottesville, the parade ground at West Point, and then your half-empty bottle of Madeira on the spindly table off-stage right. You remember your white handkerchief, slightly spotted with the wine wiped from your chin, now tucked neatly into your breast pocket to hide the purple stains from view of the audience, who can see you clearly up here stage center. Someone in that audience is coughing, nervous, repeated coughs coming from her throat, habitual and not the consequence or sign of illness. It will have a slight negative effect on your recitation, for, unless you can pick up the rhythm, the pattern of her coughing and can arrange always to be speaking at the same time, she will succeed in coughing while you are silent between stanzas or when you pause momentarily for dramatic effect, and it may have the effect of silencing you completely. You listen closely for the pattern of her coughs, and, surreptitiously, you hope, slip your watch from your vest pocket and study its face, while the Reverend Doctor Woolsey continues his lengthy introduction of the poet Edgar Poe and the unseen woman coughs, then coughs again, and, after thirty-two seconds, yet again. You calculate that if you commence reciting the poem seventeen seconds after a given cough, she will cough again in the middle of the third line and after that at the middle of every twelfth line (the 15th, 27th, 39th, etc.) and at the end of every twelfth line from the begin-

ning (the 12th, 24th, 36th, etc.). This particular spacing will mini-
mize the effect of her coughing, will make it only slightly negative.
But negative just the same, for it means that you will have to run
each of those twelfth end-stopped lines rapidly into the following
line, which will blur your every sixth rhyme and somewhat diminish
the dramatic structure of the poem. As for its effect on the raven's
harsh refrain, you can only hope that the audience is sufficiently
familiar with the poem to hear with its collective ear the croak of
Nevermore in the very coughing of the woman, as it were, as if you
Edgar Poe the poet said nothing, as if you merely mouthed the
words, for the raven, for the unseen woman in the audience coughing, for the woman in your dream, for your mother dying in an attic
room in Richmond, Virginia, your mother, whose consumptive
cough and groans and finally her very shrieks are muffled into
silence by the women in the kitchen wrapping your head with a scarf
so that you cannot hear your mother dying, will not remember this
awful time in your life, and will not remember your mother.

III

You return to the hotel, sober and alone, exchange greetings and
complaints about the midsummer heat with the desk clerk, and climb
the carpeted stairs to your room on the second floor. The recitation
went well. You overcame the woman's coughing interruptions just as
you'd planned, and at the end the audience rose and applauded with
gratitude. A few women near the front, when they rose from their
seats to thank you for reciting your "magnificent and profound"
poem, could be seen with tears washing their cheeks. Afterwards,
when you departed the stage, you discovered that someone, a janitor,
probably, had removed your half-emptied bottle of Madeira. At the
time, you took the disappearance of the bottle as a blessing and a
sign, and later, at the Reverend Doctor Woolsey's gathering for the
literary ladies and gentlemen of Richmond, Virginia, you declined
the sherry and asked for water, a glass of cool, clear water with a
bruised leaf of mint dropped into it. And so now you arrive at your
hotel room sober. But late, past midnight, for, because tonight you

were sober, you spoke to the ladies and gentlemen with a lucidity driven by logic that astonished them, made them beg you to stay and continue to mystify, enchant, and bewilder them with your de-mystification, your disenchantment, and your clarity. Man is always amazed by what is most rational, you muse to yourself as you enter your darkened room. The irrational, though it makes him feel help-less, out of control, child-like, seems more "natural" to him. You light the lamp, sit on the bed, and slowly remove your shoes. You think: And man is *right* to believe in the "naturalness" of un-reason. And right to be amazed by what is most rational, to be simulta-neously shocked and relieved by one who presents himself as de-mys-tification, disenchantment and clarity personified. Both right and *good*—for those are the modern vices we set against the ancient virtues of faith, hope and charity!

You hold your head in your cool palms. Oh my! Oh my! To aspire to purge one's mind and all its manifestations of every taint of un-reason—such an aspiration must be *blasphemy!* For to be pure reason, to be self-generating, to be unable to remember your mother—is to be a *god!* Is that why you can't remember your mother's face, her smell, her touch, her voice? Is this painful ab-sence the necessary consequence of your o'er-vaunting ambition? Evil. Evil. Your say the words aloud, over and over. Evil. Evil. You draw off your socks and your trousers, your jacket, vest, shirt, and necktie, your underclothes, all the while murmuring Evil, evil, evil.

Until at last you are naked, the poet Edgar Poe author of "The Raven," naked in the dim light of a hotel room in Richmond, Vir-ginia. You peer down at your toes, bent and battered, each toe topped with a thin wad of black hairs. Your knees, knobbed, the skin grey and crackled, and your gaunt thighs, your genitals, dry, puckered, and soft, half-covered with a smoky patch of hair. You look at your drooping belly and your navel, that primeval scar, and your breasts, like two empty pouches. You study your hands, twin nests of spiders, and your thin arms, the moles, freckles, discolor-ations, fissures, hairs, and blemishes, and your grey, slack skin.

Suddenly you try to look at your face—but you cannot. There is a dresser mirror across from you to your right a few paces, but that will not do. You want to look upon your face directly. And you cannot. You know that if you can look directly at your own face, you will be able to remember your mother's face. And then her touch, her smell, her voice. You touch your face with your fingertips, rubbing them across nose, lips, eyes, ears, and cheeks. You can get the facts of your face, but you cannot look upon it directly. Just as you can get the facts of your mother's life, from the memories of the women, those young women now old, but you cannot remember her directly yourself. Is that why you have for so many years aspired to what is evil? Because it was easier for you than to become a "natural" human being, easier than remembering your mother? Easier to be evil than good? You are weeping silently. Which is it? Are you unable to remember your mother because you are evil and persist in blasphemy, or are you evil and persist in blasphemy because you cannot remember your mother? Which? For one must be a cause, the other the effect. Which the cause? Which the effect? Why are you weeping? Why are you naked? Why are you the poet Edgar Poe author of "The Raven"? Why are you not a particular, remembered, and memorialized mother's son?

IV

In the graveyard beside the church on the hill is your mother's grave. You will depart this city in an hour by train for Baltimore. You have eaten breakfast alone in the hotel dining room and have arranged for a driver to carry you first to the church on the hill, then back into the city to the railroad station. You pay your bill, lift your satchel, and leave the hotel for the carriage waiting outside. You stop a moment on the veranda and admire the soft morning sunlight on the brick buildings and sidewalks, the elm and live oak trees that line the streets, the white dome of the capitol building a few blocks east, and beyond that, with the river between, the white spire of the church next to where your mother's body was buried nearly four decades ago. This will not be the first time you have visited your mother's grave, to stand before it with your mind mutely churning, and then, after a few moments of vertigo, to leave. You have made this pilgrimage hundreds of times, as a young boy, as an adolescent, and as a man, even in military uniform, even while drunk. And it has always been the same. From the very first time, when Mrs. Allan took you outside the church after the service one Sunday morning and walked to the graveyard and stood hand in hand with you above the freshly cut plaque laid in the ground and told you that your mother's body had been buried here, precisely here, at this spot, from that very first time until this, it has been the same for you. Silence in your ears, no noise from without, no words from within, and a feeling, painful and frightening, of falling, as if down a well that reaches to the center of the earth. Yet, despite that feeling, you have returned to this spot compulsively, like an animal driven by an instinct. You have no sense of there being a reason for it. It is as if you are drawn there by a force that originates there, not here inside your own head, among your sensations, memories, and ideas of the sanctified and holy. No, the power lies out there, in that graveyard, in that one all but unmarked grave. And now, as a middle-aged man in the middle of an illustrious career, as the poet Edgar Poe author of "The Raven," you find yourself standing once again in that cool, tree-shaded cemetery beside the old Episcopal church on the hill, and once again you descend into a well of silence. Your mind has gone mute, and you no longer hear the wind in the leaves overhead, the wagon and carriage traffic on the cobbled street behind you, the morning twitter of birds and the coo of the doves from the niches of the steeple. You look down at the grassy plot of ground before you, the tarnished plaque at your feet, and you feel yourself begin the descent. But this time, for no cause you can name, now or later, at the point of its beginning, before you have become terrified, you resist. You pull away and step back a few paces as if from a slap and you bring the entire grave into your gaze and sharply into focus, the rich green grass, the switching patterns of shadow and sunlight on the grass, the square plaque sinking into the ground at the head of the grave. You can see each individual blade of grass, even those bent and crushed beneath the feet of some passing cleric or attendant this very morning. You are still wrapped in silence, as if in a caul. You can hear nothing, nothing. And you have no thought. You watch the shadows cast on the grave by the fluttering leaves of the live oak overhead, and slowly they organize into an image, one that you yourself are surely creating as you watch, but an image which nonetheless exists in the world outside you, a configuration of shade against sunlight on the grassy plot of your mother's grave. The shades separate, move together, slowly swirl, separate, and come together again, until you begin to see the shape of a single eye, large, wide open, an extraordinary eye, a wholly familiar eye yet one you have never seen before. It resembles an eye you have seen in daguerreotypes, and in mirrors. It is the eye of a close blood relation, it is your mother's eye, it is your own eye. You stare peacefully into it, and feel it stare peacefully back. Then, gradually, the image fades, the shadows move apart, and the eye is gone from your sight. But you can remember it. You instantly recall it to your mind, as if to test the reality of the experience, and it appears there, as tender and filled with love for you as when it first appeared out of the shadows. You turn and slowly leave the cemetery. As you climb into the waiting carriage, you try once again to remember your mother, and you recall her beautiful dark eye, her loving gaze on you, her only son, her beloved child. Bathed in that gaze, you return to the city of Richmond, Virginia, so that you may leave it.

The Adjutant Bird

. . . A native-born New Englander all his life will cherish and nurture a vision of existence that probably will have been first articulated for him by Thoreau, I told her. We were in bed; her head was buried face down in her pillow, blocking out the light from the reading lamp next to me; I was staring into the whiteness of the ceiling. I'm not sure this vision is not shared with the rest of the population, I went on, but I do know that Thoreau's version of it, his particular set of images, settings, and personae, happen to be characteristic of the New Englander's American Dream so-called, whereas Southerners, Midwesterners, and Far Westerners seem to employ other sets of images, settings, and personae. At least that's my belief. Unfortunately, I can't ever know for sure, because, after all, I am a native-born New Englander and I am trying to tell about the character of my dreams as if no one had ever explained them to me before . . .

That is what I told my wife. Precisely.

But not exactly. I mean, not *actually.*

I suppose I should say that the paragraph above is indeed a direct quotation, at least insofar as memory is reliable, for it is the statement I formulated and then carefully memorized, but never really uttered, while my wife lay beside me, drifting slowly into sleep, and I lay there with *Walden* open on my belly, stared into the shadow-banked white ceiling and let myself gloom over with thoughts about my future with this woman.

Amazing—the way I inevitably seem to follow this sequence.

Anyhow, *that's* the trouble—how to explain such a future to a woman who happens to be a Southerner (or Midwesterner or Far Westerner, for that matter) and who therefore will always call a quite different situation to mind whenever the question of a future is raised.

This can be terribly frustrating—and not just to a native-born New Englander—and as a result of this frustration I usually avoid peopling my fantasies and dreams of a future with anyone known to me at this present time or at any time in the past. This de-population, or rather, re-population, of my future is not the result of any hatred or special animosity towards my wife, children, or friends. Heavens, no. As a matter of fact, I thoroughly enjoy living with these people, every one of them. It's just the frustration, mentioned above (and hereafter not to be referred to again, since that is not what I am presently concerned with; I just thought I'd mention it in passing, that's all) that gets to me. The thing I'm after here is Thoreau. Or at least it begins with Thoreau. With *Walden* and the end of chapter sixteen, to be exact. For, after formulating and memorizing for delivery to my wife the statement quoted above, I turned back to the book on my belly, which indirectly had prompted the statement in the first place, and I read again the passage quoted here below:

Thus it appears that the sweltering inhabitants of Charleston and New Orleans, of Madras and Bombay and Calcutta, drink at my well. In the morning I bathe my intellect in the stupendous and cosmogonal philosophy of the Bhagvat-Geeta. . . . I lay down the book and go to my well for water, and lo! there I meet the servant of the Brahmin, priest of Brahma and Visnu and Indra, who still sits in his temple on the Ganges reading the Vedas, or dwells at the root of a tree with his crust and water jug. I meet his servant come to draw water for his master, and our buckets as it were grate together in the same well. The pure Walden water is mingled with the sacred water of the Ganges. With the favoring winds it is wafted past the site of the fabulous islands of Atlantis and the Hesperides, makes the periplus of Hanno, and, floating by Ternate and Tidore and the mouth of the Persian Gulf, melts in the tropic gales of the Indian seas, and is landed in ports of which Alexander only heard the names.

He's talking about ice here. Ice! Hard white Massachusetts ice—brought in coffin-sized blocks from Walden Pond, Fresh Pond, Crystal Lake, and half a dozen other Boston and Concord ponds and lakes, dragged into Boston proper on pungs "by a hundred Irishmen with Yankee overseers" straight out to Gray's Wharf, where the one-hundred-fifty-pound blocks were packed into the bottom of one of Frederick Tudor's ice ships. The blocks, incidentally, were packed first in sawdust, home-grown Yankee pine sawdust—after Tudor had first tried, and failed, to keep the ice from melting in the hold by wrapping it in rice, and then wheat chaff, then hay, tanbark, and even coal dust brought up from Philadelphia. But that's not important, and it shoves me somewhat ahead of myself.

The important thing is the spreading of the dream, the idyll, like a stain, or, more appropriately, like quickly melting snow, from Thoreau's cabin on Walden Pond to Frederick Tudor at Gray's Wharf, who stands in the cutting wind that knifes in from the Bay, pacing nervously up and down behind the clerk on the high stool, who counts, counts, counts, 160, 170, 180 tons of New England ice catalogued and tagged for Calcutta.

At this point in my reflections, I reached over my wife's inert body to the switch on the wall above her head and snapped off the light next to me, and, settling comfortably into the darkness, I tried to remember all that I knew about Frederick Tudor and his East Indies ice trade. I did not get out of bed to write these notes until I had recalled, isolated, and then reconnected, to each other as well as to the entire body of information, all the data that follow. (I might add that I have attempted to place the data in chronological sequence here, rather than trying to duplicate my original train of thought, which of course was in a sequence determined by the idiosyncratic turns and jumps of memory.)

To begin with, then, Frederick Tudor in 1805, at the age of twenty-two, was the first person to propose ice, New England's best-known environmental liability (rocks and boulders, glacial till, run second), as a commodity for trade with ports and peoples in the tropical regions. His first attempt was a disaster. That first time, 130 tons of ice, cut from his father's pond in Saugus and shipped to Martinique, melted somewhere south of Chesapeake Bay, and the water-filled ship, foundering like a bathtub, nearly went down off Hatteras. Tudor wrote in his *Journal* as follows: "He who gives back at the first repulse, and without striking the second blow despairs of success, has never been, is not now, and never will be a hero in love, war, or business."

About this time he realized that if the nearby farmers in Reading, Medford, and Lynn could keep their houses and barns insulated in winter by packing the buildings up to the windows in sawdust, he should be able to insulate his ice blocks with the very same material. Which he did—after first having the carrying vessels double sheathed and his captains instructed to keep the hatches tightly shut at all times, no matter what. A hatch left ajar would fill the hold with fresh lake water almost overnight.

By 1812 Tudor had a small West Indies trade built up, a trade that got wiped out completely by the War. But with the Peace of Ghent he asked for and received exclusive government permission to construct ice houses at Kingston and Havana, and, with the advantage provided by monopoly, he was able by 1817 to move his trade into Savannah, Charleston, and New Orleans.

I can't remember when he made his first attempt to gain the South American ports, but I suspect that it wasn't until the late '20's. Nevertheless, it was a man named Osgood Carney, supercargo for the first voyage to Rio de Janeiro in the barque *Madagascar,* who was instructed from Boston by Tudor in this manner: "If you can make a commencement for introducing the habit of cold drinks *at the same price as warm* and at the *ordinary* drinking places, even if you *give* the ice, you will do well. The shops frequented by the lowest people are the ones to be chosen for this purpose." Where before there had existed only ignorance, an absence, Tudor had been able to create a need, a presence. Also, once Carney had managed to convince the hospitals of Rio that they needed New England ice, a request was made to the government of Brazil—on the grounds of Tudor ships being necessary to public health—for a remission of all import duties and all export duties on products (mainly hides) carried out of Rio on Tudor ships. The request, naturally, was rejected, but not without some very serious consideration on the part of the Brazilian officials. This gives you an idea of how clearly Tudor's mind worked.

Then in May, 1833, came Tudor's first attempt to sell ice in the Far East. He shipped 180 tons of it aboard the *Tuscany,* Captain Littlefield, instructing the captain something like this: "As soon as you have arrived in latitude 12° north, you will have carried ice as far south as it has ever been carried before, and your ship becomes then a Discovery Ship, and as such, I feel confident that you will do everything for the eventual success of the undertaking. . . ." Captain Littlefield arrived in Calcutta with two-thirds of his cargo intact— that is, still in its solid state—which, at the time, was thought a considerable feat. His return freight was handled by the Indian firms of Bubu Rajkissen Mitter and Jamsetjee, Jeejeebhoy & Co.—on the banks of the Hooghly River.

By 1841, then, Frederick Tudor was a wealthy, highly honored merchant, and he was able to pay back easily the quarter-million dollars in debts that he had incurred by his earlier failed attempts to sell ice where no ice grew.

Miscellaneous bits of information still cling to my thoughts, and so I place them here, at the end, for their own sake:

At Charleston, South Carolina, in 1834, Tudor, because of growing competition from the Thayer Brothers of Boston, was selling ice for only 1 1/4 cents per pound. The Thayers could not meet his price reduction, however, and soon turned to swapping Lynn shoes for California hides.

At New Orleans, at the same time, he was getting two cents per pound for ice that cost him but $435 per brig load (160 to 180 tons, depending on how they stacked it). And in 1833 in Rio de Janeiro he could sell twelve pounds of his ice for one Spanish dollar.

That brings me up to the present . . .

Except to note that my title for these notes comes from Kipling's *Second Jungle Book,* where there's a quick reference to the adjutant bird, which, swallowing "a piece of white stuff" thrown at him by a white man in a boat on the Ganges, is said by Kipling to have swallowed "a seven-pound lump of Wareham Lake ice, off an American ice-ship." I'm assuming, or have assumed, that the boat was Tudor's and that the ice came from a pond on my property, or one just like it, or possibly even Thoreau's. My wife would never understand this. But I don't care. I'm happy.

The New World

The Puritan, however, like a memento mori grinning from a mirror, is still among us. Relentlessly, he reminds himself and us of our longings to shatter his image with the possibility of rebirth, of conversion, of utter transformation. And now, after tens of generations of staring stubbornly into himself, as if into the white night of the Arctic, at last there comes a dawn when, though he continues to die for transformation, he is no longer quite so terrified of its implicit lawlessness, and it occurs to the Puritan that all along he has been averting his eyes. He wobbles on his pivot and finds himself seeking the possibility of transformation elsewhere. And this precise moment, this wobbling, is what begins the tale of Bernardo de Balbuena and Mosseh Alvares, the poet and the goldsmith, Catholic prelate and exiled Jew, minor epic and forgotten parable.

There are, then, two heroes in this tale, neither of them particularly heroic. The first of the pair, Bernardo de Balbuena, born almost five centuries ago in an age and place of Spanish-speaking giants, was a man of diminutive proportions, although he is in fact a figure whose personal and public histories are even today available to anyone who, for whatever reasons, might wish to know them. For, while the author assumes that the reader of his tale is a person who does not possess any overriding desire to know these histories personal and public, nevertheless, if one or two or some small number of one's readers do in fact possess such a peculiar turn of mind as to want to immerse themselves in the data and the moribund literary expressions of a man long dead who was a second-rate epic poet and a middle-level Church bureaucrat in the far provinces, they ought to consider themselves singled out now and released from all obligations to continue reading here.[1] Unfortunately for such readers, the personal and public histories of one's second hero, Mosseh Alvares, a Sephardic goldsmith who, in the early seventeenth century, happened to be residing in the very town where Balbuena was presiding as abbot, are more resistant to the probes of scholarship. A scholar would have difficulty proving that the man existed at all, though (if the scholar wished it) one could help out by pointing him in the direction of a faded and pitted slate gravestone in the Jewish graveyard in present-day Spanish Town, then called Villa de la Vega, on the island of Jamaica. One could also direct him to several excellent and well-catalogued private collections of seventeenth-century jewelry. One could even send him to the Metropolitan Museum of Art in New York City, where, at a recent exhibit entitled "Caribbean Gold," he could have gazed upon an intricately engraved egg-shaped pendant of moss agate and pearl with a foil-like gilt frame and fine link chain.

If the scholar followed such directions as these, however, he'd only lose the way. He'd lose track of the plottings this tale is attempting to map, plottings which, when their grids are finally drawn, will reveal the moral topography of at least two particular lives, and, one hopes, more than two.

To begin with, one might well consider the abbot's idea about ideas. For Bernardo de Balbuena, the possible lives that faced a particular man were as many and as various as that man's ideas for a

[1] There are, for the released reader, the excellent and thorough *Bernardo de Balbuena* by J. Rojas Garciduenas (Mexico City, 1958); *"El Bernardo" of Bernardo de Balbuena: A Study of the Poem with Particular Attention to its Relations to the Epics of Boiardo and Ariosto and to its Significance in the Spanish Renaissance,* by John Van Horne (Urbana, Ill., 1927); *Bernardo de Balbuena, Biografía y Crítica* (Guadalajara, 1940), also by Van Horne; and the execrably written but lovingly researched series of articles by Sylvia Wynter, "Bernardo de Balbuena, Epic Poet and Abbot of Jamaica, 1562–1627," *Jamaica Journal,* Vol. 3, nos. 3 and 4; Vol. 4, nos, 1 and 3. And, of course, there are always Balbuena's own writings, *Obras Completas* (Madrid, 1945).

life. Thus a person was not merely *capable* of inventing his life (which is not the same as "making it up"); he had no choice. It was his destiny. One should say, It was his Destiny. So that whatever way a man ended up living and, at the very end, dying, there was no way he could avoid the responsibility for having invented both.

Balbuena's idea about ideas was not, of course, new, and as long as he was careful to express himself with sufficient respect for ecclesiastical, philosophical, political, and scientific conventions of terminology and dramatization, the idea was in no way heretical. Which was fortunate for Balbuena, for he was, in all the ways of possible advancement in the world, ambitious.

Most people, then and there as much as here and now, claim not to believe that they are responsible for having invented their lives. One's friends and neighbors speak, variously, of God's Will, determinism, behavior modification, fate, destiny, and so forth; but regardless, what they are trying to do is draw a portrait of man that mirrors their carefully, deliberately, if not consciously, already invented image, or idea, of man. As Balbuena said, "We choose our destinies."

Now, what interests one about Balbuena is that, throughout a life that was deeply dissatisfying to him, he nonetheless persisted in resisting an easy and, at that time, a popular determinism to explain it. In fact, when he wrote "We choose our destinies" to Spain's greatest poet and playwright, his personal friend Lope de Vega, he used the sentence to sentence himself, as it were, to a life that, up to then, had caused him half a century of profound frustration and joyless, thankless labor.

One imagines Balbuena in Jamaica. He is forty-nine years old, bookish, nearsighted, arthritic (the consequences of four round-trip sea voyages between the New World and the Old to further his entwined careers as churchman and epic poet). He owns an impressive number of leather-bound volumes and two servants, half-breed Tlaxcalan Indian boys who have been with him since his Guadalahara days and who, with his books, have accompanied him on the four sea voyages back and forth between the Caribbean and Madrid. He owns the manuscript of *El Bernardo,* his as yet unpublished epic poem, and the appointment to the abbacy in Jamaica, an appointment that places him, with great reluctance, in charge of hardly more than half a thousand Christian souls in a poor chunk of wilderness. At this juncture, Mosseh Alvares, the Jewish goldsmith, is but a statistic in Balbuena's life as a bureaucrat. For Balbuena, Alvares lives only in the census that, in compliance with the terms of his appointment, he conducted upon his arrival in Jamaica. From this census, one learns that the total number of inhabitants on the island in 1611 was 1,510 and of this number 523 were Spanish (Christian) men and women, with 173 Spanish (Christian) children, and 75 were what Balbuena called "foreigners" (Spanish and Portuguese Jews). Alvares was somewhere among these. Of the original inhabitants, the Arawak Indians, called by Balbuena "the natives of the island," there were only 74, down from the 10,000 estimated to have resided in Jamaica a hundred years earlier. Additionally, there were 107 "free Negroes" and 558 enslaved Negroes.[2]

Jamaica was a stagnating backwater. A century after discovery, it still languished like a tidal pool deserted by the irresistible swell of empire. The Spanish gold, the shipping and transshipping industries, the universities, cathedrals, and monasteries, the publishers and the wealthy and elegant intelligentsia—in short, everything that could be regarded as being of lifelong value to a middle-aged, clerical *literatus* stuck in the back corner of the Caribbean—all these things were off in the Old World or were elsewhere in the New, were in Hispaniola, Puerto Rico, Mexico City, were even, alas, in Lima.

Balbuena, after ten years of highly praised service to the church in the outpost of Guadalajara, had asked for an appointment as abbot, if not bishop, to Mexico City, San Juan, and Lima, in that order. (After Guadalajara, an ambitious man had no choice but to seek

---

[2] Sylvia Wynter claims that there were doubtless many more Arawaks and ex-slaves who had escaped by this time into the mountain fastness in the center of the island and who were already settling into the patterns of guerrilla warfare against the Europeans that would characterize the life of the so-called Maroons for the next two hundred years; nevertheless, she is convinced that Balbuena's census for the European inhabitants (Christian and Jewish) and the enslaved Arawaks and Africans is correct.

these posts, or he would not be thought ambitious and thus would not be trusted with any difficult task.) To help effect that end, he had, as mentioned, traveled several times to Madrid. But also he had dedicated *El Bernardo,* the product of his ten years' labor while a parish priest in Guadalajara, to the Count of Lemos, who was president of the council that governed the Indies. Further, Balbuena had seeded the enormous poem with lines guaranteed to ensure the Count's immortality, such as,

> The New World, unworthy of your favor,
> Adores you with the voice and livery of man,
> Your noble blood, descended from a thousand kings,
> Sends just laws and honors to that land . . . .
>
> —Book I, stanza 3

Later in the poem, doubtless hoping to define forever their special relationship, the poet had named the Count

> . . . a new Augustus who showers
> Honors on men of letters . . .
>
> —Book XX, stanza 84

Beyond this sacrifice (for surely he was not ashamed of the dedication and the lines quoted above), he'd borrowed large sums of money from individuals not of his family, and he'd used up several years in Madrid diligently lobbying for the appointment, so that when in 1608 it finally arrived and turned out to be not a bishopric, but an abbacy, and not in Mexico City or San Juan or even Lima, but in Jamaica, he was by then too old, too poor, and too compromised not to receive it with seeming gratitude. For two more years he dawdled in Madrid, talking poetry with friends and trying to devise a way to raise enough money to repay his debts, and then, apparently still owing huge sums, he assumed his post, as if it were an unwanted but inevitable fate.

Even so, one must admire his intellectual integrity (or persistence), for it was not long after he'd arrived in Villa de la Vega and been installed as abbot in a rude, mid-afternoon ceremony at St. Iago's, the tiny village church in the center of the only collection of buildings on Jamaica that could in any way be designated a town, that, in the now

famous letter to Lope de Vega, he wrote, "We choose our destinies."
    Perhaps it was that very evening, December 11, 1610, when, fa-
tigued, filled to his blue eyes with not altogether cheering
impressions of the place and people (Alvares not yet even a statistic
in his official life), the short, thick-bodied, balding poet who only
happened to be an abbot—or was he an abbot who only happened to
be a poet?—sat himself down at the wobbly refectory table in his
chamber and, to the noise of cicadas, crickets, frogs, roosters, and
dogs, the bray of a donkey and laugh of a goat, he put pen to ink and
ink to parchment and tried to unburden and clarify his overbur-
dened and muddled heart by writing to Spain's greatest poet, who
only happened to be his closest friend—or was it his closest friend
who only happened to be Spain's greatest poet?
    Regardless, "I am astonished," Balbuena wrote, "by the actions
of the men, and also even the women here, European as well as
Negro—not including the Jews, however, of which, thanks to Columbus and his grasping lineage, there are quite a number here, keeping
all their pagan rituals and esoteric ways. All the others, however,
quite openly relieve themselves against the sides of buildings, in
courtyards, and even, like dogs, against trees, bushes, and shrubs.
Even in Guadalajara, such a practice would have been thought ugly.
Here, however, it seems to be thought normal. Most of what would
be thought ugly elsewhere is here regarded as normal. This, I suppose, is what is meant by the 'New World.' One fervently prays not.
But the aforementioned public urination, and defecation as well, is
an example of what is normal here. Also such things as cattle and
swine slain only for their hides, stripped of their skins and left to
stink and rot in the sun, hundreds at a time. Additionally, though I
have been here but a few weeks, I have already seen men copulate
with goats, trees, and even holes in the moist ground, though none
reveals these things to me in confession. Incest here is more usual
than relations between husband and wife. The people, white as well
as black, Christian as much as pagan, are greedy, lazy, corpulent,
diseased, ignorant, indolent of mind and spirit, and in all ways
behave in ways other than what, thank God, would be called
'normal' anywhere else in this world, New or Old. Yet they remain

normal here. Which is doubtless why the people prefer being here to anywhere else—and, except for the Jews, such is true of them, for they do prefer life here to possibilities of life anywhere else. Ah, my friend, it appears again, even in this desperate, lonely, bleak land, that we choose our destinies."

An indirect reference above to the presence of Mosseh Alvares in Jamaica can be explained in this way: Mosseh Alvares was the great-grandson of one José Alvares, also a goldsmith, who had arrived in Jamaica from Spain by way of Amsterdam in 1531. In March, 1492, as is well known among Jews even today, the Jews living in Spain had been given the so-called choice of either being baptized as Christian or departing forever from all Spanish dominions. Between 200,000 and 400,000 Jews chose to leave, many of them for northern Europe, many for the New World, specifically to Portuguese Brazil (where they stayed until 1640, when Spain took it over) and Jamaica, which, in the sixteenth and seventeenth centuries, was possibly the only place left in the world where Spanish was spoken and yet was not a part of the Spanish Empire, at least not officially. This was because the island of Jamaica, once it had been determined that there was no gold there, had been presented to Christopher Columbus, his reward for having discovered the New World. It was thus his private fiefdom and, thanks to the persistence and legal perspicacity of what Balbuena called the Admiral's "grasping lineage," it remained more or less under the rule of the Columbus family in an almost medieval way for another hundred and fifty years, until, in 1655, the English simply took the island away. In fact, according to Spanish law, Jamaica is still the private property of the descendants of Christopher Columbus. Balbuena, incidentally, was the last abbot to be appointed for Jamaica by the Council in the Indies. Afterwards, even this prerogative was given over, and his successor was appointed by the Duke de Veragua, Marquis of Jamaica and heir to the legacy of his ancestor, Don Cristobal Colon de Caravajal y Moroto (Christopher Columbus).

End of digression. One continues to imagine Balbuena in Jamaica. The abbot closes his letter, "I remain, etc.," folds and seals it, places it at the far right corner of the table and withdraws from the drawer

at his belly the several sheets of paper which are "The Prologue" to
El Bernardo. This, plus two eight-line stanzas, will be the only parts
of his poem that he will write during his ten years of residence in
Jamaica. Every night, month after month, year after year, the abbot,
before he goes to bed, will pull out the pages of "The Prologue" or
some one or another of the twenty-four books of his epic, and he will
read through what he has written, changing a comma here, an
article there, correcting the spelling, adjusting the meters and the
rhymes, going back over his tiny alterations again and again, so
many times that frequently he will change them back to what they
were when he first set them down in Guadalajara a decade or more
earlier.

His nightly habit, for the years of his residency in Jamaica, will be
to read through fifty or a hundred of the more than forty thousand
lines of the poem, then to sip a glass of sacramental wine on the veranda, and then (not forgetting a brief prayer at the side of his bed
before he climbs, sighing, in) to sleep.

The poem will languish unpublished—though not unread, for
Balbuena had been able to circulate a manuscript copy among the
best literary and political circles in Madrid during his stay there—
until after the abbot has left Jamaica to assume, at long last, the
crosier and miter of Bishop of San Juan. By then, however, he will no
longer think of himself as a poet. His intertwined twin careers will
have disentangled themselves from each other, and he will be
described as a wealthy man. The Puerto Rican chronicler Diego
Torres de Vargas, in his account of the island of Puerto Rico published in 1647, will write, concerning the abbot, that "to the afore-
said Don Pedro de Solier succeeded Doctor Bernardo de Balbuena,
Abbot of Jamaica, from whence he came wealthy from the exchange
of coinage between the several colonies." And, of course, as Bishop
of San Juan, he will be an extremely powerful man.

But he will enjoy both descriptions. And he will not long to write
another epic poem. "One is enough for any man," he will write,
again, to Lope de Vega, not mentioning, naturally, that his years as
abbot in Jamaica and his apparent skill as a swimmer upon the fluc-
tuating tides of currency rates will have made him wealthy (for Lope

was one of the people back in Madrid to whom he still owed large sums of money). These years and activities will have altered his destiny. An intelligent and evidently quite conscious man, as well as a man of enormous intellectual integrity, especially now that he will have succeeded in rising to what he always regarded as his proper place in the Church's hierarchical ladder, Balbuena will dutifully observe the change in his destiny, will observe that he is now an old man nearing the end of his life, and he will be brave enough to admit that he chose that change.

"I am conscious," he will write to his old friend, "of having become a man of some means and considerable force in the world, and now that you are seeing my life's poem into print, I will doubtless soon be a man of some fame as well. I confess it, I wanted all this. From the start, I wanted it.

"I did not want to be alone, however. Nor did I wish to consume my life alone in a rude land. Yet, to be fair to God Almighty and to the dictates of history, I do not know how else I could have obtained the power and now the fame I so hungered for. Is this not, after all, what my poem is struggling to demonstrate? Am I not El Bernardo himself? I was not born to wealth, power, and fame, as so many others were. You know that. I chose them. And for that I needed the New World. I will not now complain, as my life here begins to close, that I do not possess what I never had the wisdom to seek in the first place."

The Puritan among us may not comprehend such a letter, but surely Lope de Vega did. After all, he was familiar with the poem, *El Bernardo*, and reading his old friend's question, "Am I not El Bernardo himself?" he could fold the letter, peer wearily across his chamber to the thick, dust-covered manuscript, and murmur to himself, "Oh, yes, yes, indeed you are." The Puritan would be disgusted, perhaps; but Lope would be cheered. The Puritan would call it self-evading vanity; Lope would call it self-discovering transformation (at the least, Lope would believe in that possibility; the Puritan would only *want* to believe).

Mosseh Alvares, the goldsmith, would never have read the letter, of course, nor would he have known of the existence of the poem.

But even so, he, too, would have understood and forgiven the abbot for his poem. After all, he was an image-maker himself, was he not? "Look, he's not so bad," the goldsmith once said to his daughter Rachel. "It's all right that he's a Gentile, and an abbot, even. He's still a man. And a man suffers."

The abbot, who throughout his tenure in Jamaica had been Alvares' best customer, his only customer, practically, had just left the shop. His robed figure was picking its way carefully up the rocky slope to the church. At the door of the shop Rachel, scraping paraffin from her palms, scowled after him. "He's a pig!" she hissed. "You saw how he looked at me!"

Alvares stared at his sandaled feet. He knew that he should feel shame for not feeling anger, but he could feel neither emotion. "You don't understand," he finally said in a low voice. And he was right, for the daughter did not understand either man, not the abbot and not her own father, especially the ways in which the two old men were alike. Mosseh peered out the door of the tiny shop, slowly inhaled the heat and light of noon, exhaled and peered skyward, when he caught sudden sight of a brace of turkey buzzards floating noiselessly overhead. They looped and cruised in circles and long, slow arcs, their wings spread, motionless, above the fast-rising currents of warm air. Those buzzards, Mosseh thought, they're like the eyes of a bad conscience—you never notice them until you've offended yourself, until a part of you has become a piece of dead meat, and then you look up, as if for forgiveness, and there they are, looping blackly, silently, overhead, between you and the God who alone can forgive you.

The old man, gaunt, grey bearded, turned and looked up along the blonde, rocky slope to the small stone church at the top, St. Iago's. There, at the door to the church, also peering at the pair of buzzards, stood the abbot. After a few seconds, the abbot let his gaze drop back from the sky, and, seeing the figure of the goldsmith below, waved slowly, and then entered the cool nave of the church.

There were many things that bound the two men together, some of them obvious to anyone who knew both men, some of them known only to the men themselves, some known to no one. The two were of approximately the same age, and they both felt themselves to be cultured men who, because of the provinciality of the place they were obliged to live in, were not properly appreciated for their culture. Also, they were both, in the ways of their respective worlds, ambitious, the abbot as churchman and literary figure, the Jew as artisan and articulate member of the Jewish community.

Alvares, as much as Balbuena, believed that what we make of our lives is merely the fleshly expression of our idea of what's possible. Both men saw life as a philosophical activity—though, of course, neither of them, since he had never strictly been asked, would have put it quite that way. After all, Balbuena was a father in the Church, and Alvares believed himself to be a dedicated carrier of his people's inherited and revealed law.

"If God had not invented the Jews," the goldsmith said from the door, saying it as if to his daughter but in reality saying it for himself, trying it out as a possible description of the world he'd found himself in, "then the Jews," he went on, meaning himself, "would have invented Him." He sighed again and shuffled back into the cool darkness of the cluttered shop.

Rachel, long limbed, dark eyed, olive skinned, a beauty, looked at her father with a slight frown. She was less and less sure, as he grew older, that he was orthodox, though naturally he asserted that he was indeed orthodox, the most orthodox of all the seventy-five Jews residing in Jamaica. They had no rabbi to meet their spiritual and cultural needs (the last one had died seven years prior to the arrival of the abbot, after having eaten improperly prepared cassava), and by default these tasks and definitions had fallen to Mosseh. Thus, among his people he functioned in much the same way that Balbuena functioned among the Christians.

But there was still more that united the two old men. They were in the same place in the New World at the same time in the history of the Old World, and, in a deep way, they were there for the same reasons. As a result, they experienced many of the same ambivalent emotions in their lives. They both were proud of their accomplishments under duress, but they resented the duress. They both were grateful to be situated where they were in life, but they were hurt and angry that they could not be better situated. And they both had imagined idealized versions of themselves—Balbuena his Bernardo, and Alvares his Patriarch. This last, the Patriarch, appears at the center of most of the parables and allegories that Alvares employed to enforce his role as *chachon,* as moral and cultural arbiter of his people on the island. The character called the Patriarch, as much like Alvares and unlike him as El Bernardo was like and unlike Balbuena, was at the center of the tale that the goldsmith, from his stool at his workbench, began that noontime to relate to his daughter, Rachel.

From interior evidence, it seems clear that, while the tale was told first ("first" in the historical sense) by the old goldsmith, told first and often to his fellow Jews in exile as a complex moral lesson, the man could not have invented it. However, there are indications that its use as a mere parable was soon exhausted, or else, because of its moral subtlety, the story became gradually incomprehensible, even to those who went on retelling and listening to the tale after Alvares had died. For after him, with each new telling, it began to be embellished and elaborated upon, a turn of phrase here, a new detail there, and also cut, pared, so that what finally remained, even within fifteen years of the first circulation of the tale in Jamaica (which seems to have been around the time Balbuena had become unexpectedly wealthy, around 1619 or 1620), was not so much a parable or allegory as it was a true and autonomous metaphor, a kind of golden calf, if you will, that served no specifically moral purpose but was told and retold nevertheless, as if it were an object of worship being passed fervently and reverently from the hands of one rapt worshipper to another.[3]

---

[3] Though the version that follows is as close to the original as modern literary scholarship will permit, the curious reader, who may wish to trace the progeny of the story, is directed to the anthologies, *The Living Tongue: Tale-Telling as a Discipline of Thought,* by G. Wolcott Leavis (London, 1951); *Tales of Old Jamaica,* by Clinton V. Black (London, 1966); *Walking the Spanish Main,* by George Sylvester Huggins (Kingston, 1974); and *Exiles in Paradise,* by Abraham Singer (New York, 1975). See also two seldom-performed operas, *La Juive,* music by Jacques François Halévy, and *Les Huguenots,* music by Giacomo Meyerbeer, both libretti by Augustin Eugène Scribe (*La Juive* first produced in Paris, February 23, 1835; *Les Huguenots* in Paris, February 29, 1836).

Mosseh's version of the tale, in later versions commonly entitled "The Patriarch," concerns a Jew, a goldsmith residing in the city of Santa Martina, the capital of the province of Santa Martina in a far, mountainous corner of the Empire (presumably the Spanish Empire, though this is never made explicit). The story also concerns the goldsmith's daughter, Rachel, and two powerful Christian men, a bishop and a duke, and a Christian princess. The goldsmith's name was Benjamin, and the story usually begins with Benjamin, with what looks like reckless courage, deciding to keep his shop open on a day that the Bishop has decreed is a holiday, Santa Martina's Day.

Perhaps Benjamin had simply forgotten that the city was practically the Bishop's own; perhaps he had anticipated that in Santa Martina there were numerous others like him, Jews who would feel no particular obligation to close up their shops and light candles on a Christian holiday. After all, he surely didn't expect the shoemaker, the butcher, or the carpet-seller, all of whom lived in his block in the city and all of whom were Christian, to lock up their shops on his Jewish holidays. So why should they or anyone else expect him to do anything unusual on Santa Martina's Day?

Outside his door, his Gentile neighbors screamed their reasoning at him. It was because Santa Martina was the city's patron saint. It was because she had bled from her hands and her forehead right here on these streets. It was because they were proud of their patron saint, for in fact she had become the patron saint for the province itself and was rumored to be on her way to becoming the patron saint for the whole empire. Santa Martina, they shouted through the door, was what had made their city an important place to be a citizen, so if he, the Jew, were not ashamed of being a citizen here, he should close his shop today and join the rest of them in honoring her.

The people outside, by now an angry mob—even though most of them Benjamin counted as friends, customers, neighbors, and even a few of them Jewish—banged on his grill, shook their fists at him, spat on his sign, and one monkey-faced youth went so far as to defecate on a shingle and slide it into the shop.

But the goldsmith was a patient man who knew his own mind. He removed the offensive gift and then walked out to face the mob, where, standing in the middle of the cobbled street, he informed them that he loved the city of Santa Martina as much as they, but it might as well be named after a Mongol general for all he was concerned, for he was a Jew, and therefore it was forbidden for him to honor a Christian saint, no matter that he happened to love the city that had been named after her. Joseph, his apprentice, had been given leave to take the day off, Benjamin explained to the crowd, but the youth had chosen on his own to stay inside the shop and work at his and his daughter's side. This Benjamin told the crowd so they would know he was not forcing anyone else to behave and believe as he did, except, of course, for his daughter, which was accepted.

Many of the citizens, however, had accused the Jew of oppressing his apprentice, Joseph, because Joseph was a Christian, or at least he wore a gold cross around his muscular neck. They knew nothing else about him, which was natural, for, in fact, unknown to anyone, even to Benjamin and Rachel, Joseph was actually Duke José de Veragua, Marquis of Santa Martina, whose ancient claim to the Emperor's throne, it had been recently rumored, was being sponsored by the Bishop. Joseph was the Duke in disguise.

A month earlier, while shopping around town for gold earrings, the Duke had strolled into Benjamin's shop and had caught a glimpse of Rachel, and, because of the violence of his emotions, he had decided to confront these emotions and explore them to their limits. He was an honorable man, or at least he so regarded himself, and he was engaged to be married shortly to the Princess Maria de Caravajal y Moroto, a woman who was an extremely powerful figure at court, but who was kind and beautiful as well. However, the Duke, once he had seen Rachel and had realized what a mere glimpse could do, knew that he could not marry the Princess, not if he was in love with another, especially if that other was the daughter of a humble Jewish artisan.

He assured himself that if, upon examination, it turned out that he was actually in love with this girl, he would kill himself. It seemed the only reasonable thing to do, and the Duke was well known for his ability to reason well. He had spent four years at a German university, and he had also studied with Greek mathematicians. He would be sure to live up to his reputation at a time like this, for what else, he reasoned, was an ability to reason well good for, but a time like this? Thus, he had decided to disguise himself as an out-of-work apprentice and to place himself in as close proximity to Rachel as was possible, so as to determine whether or not he was truly in love with her.

Luckily, Benjamin needed a healthy, intelligent young man that season, and since there were no Jewish men available just then who were willing to train to become goldsmiths (they were all in the university in the capital, it seemed, training to become lawyers, navigators, diplomats), Benjamin agreed to take on the Gentile, who called himself Joseph, Joseph Orgo.

For a few days Benjamin groused about the shop, grumbling that none of the Jewish fathers were bringing their sons up to respect the ancient crafts, but before long Joseph was able to impress his master with his intelligence, self-discipline, and strength, also his delicacy and willingness to learn. Rachel, of course, working alongside such a man, fell deeply in love with him, for he was also a good talker, although this was a skill he wisely kept hidden from the father.

Benjamin was aware of the sensual weakness of the young, naturally, but he believed he could avoid a disaster merely by warning his daughter every night of the basic insufficiency of Gentile husbands. He told her of their drinking habits, their superstitions, their unconscious hatred of Jews, their ignorance, their historical superficiality, and so on, convinced that, because all these characteristics were self-evident, like small ears or a protruding upper lip, he was preventing his daughter from turning her fragile young life into a heap of wreckage.

Besides, he admired his daughter's good sense. She reminded him of her mother, whose memory had become for him a sacred grove. And, too, he knew how much the young woman loved him, how she would never do anything that would hurt him, any more than he would do anything that would hurt her. Families can be sustained by tens of generations on delusions such as that, before a single violation, a single broken heart, tosses every delusion away and turns the family bitterly against itself, whereupon another ten generations of cynical despair will pursue them, before new delusions and trusts can take hold and guide them. At this moment in its long history, Benjamin's family had reached the point where it could support the delusion of mutual trust and genetic good sense only under the best of circumstances, only if circumstances were gentle, smooth, soft, and slow—which of course was not the case, not with a Gentile Duke disguised as an apprentice working alongside the daughter Rachel, not with a man who was both in love with her and at the same time was engaged to marry a Gentile Princess, all this coming at a time of political crisis for Benjamin, a crisis that had erupted solely because he was a Jew living in a city that was controlled by a splenetic, self-righteous, possibly mad Bishop. What a sad time to trust family traditions of mutual affection and good sense!

Thus, when the Princess Maria de Caravajal y Moroto appeared at his door on the afternoon of Santa Martina's Day, a mere half-hour after the mob had grumpily dispersed, the goldsmith heartily congratulated himself for having kept his shop open, for, as it turned out, there was to be a ball at the palace that evening and Benjamin's shop was the only place in town where one could buy gifts or jewelry for the ball. The Princess smiled and told Benjamin that she was very glad he had remained open and she was going to run right back to the palace and let the other women know.

Her teeth were certainly the most beautiful, white, and even teeth Benjamin had ever seen. Also, he noted, she had one of those long, slender, smooth-skinned necks that make a man purse his lips and swallow a lot of air. Benjamin happily rushed into the back room and started carting out trays of stock—necklaces, bracelets, dinner rings, combs, mirrors, elaborately decorated fans, pendants, all his stock, excitedly explaining to Rachel and Joseph that the Princess Maria de Caravajal y Moroto was in the shop and was buying for the ball and his was the only shop open in the entire city of Santa Martina!

Rachel was gleeful, of course. But Joseph was not, for it was at this very moment that he entered upon the period of his moral confusion that no amount of university training seemed to have prepared him for. He peeked out the door into the front of the shop and saw the Princess, his fiancée. She was quite beautiful. He hadn't seen her for a month, having explained that he was on a secret mission in the far north that he simply could not tell her about. And to make matters worse, she was looking at a tray of men's rings, talking generously and lovingly of a gift she wanted to give her husband-to-be. Joseph stared down at his ringless, newly callused apprentice's hands and imagined them covered with beautiful rings chosen for him by his wife.

Catching himself about to groan, he whispered instead to Rachel that he had to leave, and, as he stripped off his apron and grabbed his jacket, he asked her to explain to her father that he wanted to go and light a candle for Santa Martina now, so that he could come back later and help out when the rush began, for, after the Princess had gotten back to the palace and sent all her lady friends down for jewelry and gifts for the ball, there surely was going to be some kind of rush.

Rachel understood and sneaked a kiss to his tiny ear, and the man darted out the back door without saying anything more, having already determined to return to his former life and somehow, later, to explain to this good young woman that, while he loved her deeply, he did not love her exclusively, and, because of the mitigating conditions of class, religion, and previous commitments, he reluctantly must marry another, whom he also loved, but similarly not exclusively, which was what he had needed to learn, what he had suspected might be true when he had first seen her, Rachel, and had been so taken with her that he had been compelled by honor as well as by reason to determine what in fact was the nature of his love for the daughter of the goldsmith, and now, after an invaluable, deep experience of a month, he had learned a great deal, had learned that what he hoped was *not* true (i.e., that a man could love several women equally, and thus conditions of class, religion, politics, family, etc., were of paramount significance, were, in point of fact, a man's fate) indeed *was* true, and now he would have to accept the dictates of that learning experience and mediate between what he desired to be true of love and what in the end was true of his life—that is, he was now forced, by reason, to marry the Princess Maria de Caravajal y Moroto.

It turned out that the Princess purchased no rings. The one piece of jewelry she did buy from Benjamin had to be altered so that it would be appropriate for a man's as well as a woman's neck—for she had selected an egg-shaped, ornately framed pendant with a chain too short to fit around a muscular man's muscular neck, and her plan was to wear the pendant herself until the Duke returned from his secret mission in the north, at which time she wanted to be seen in public removing the gold, agate, and pearl pendant from her own neck and placing it around his. It was a moment in the stream of time to which, through the carefully imagined and choreographed use of jewelry, she wanted to give articulation, transcendent, expressive articulation, that she knew would transform the moment into something memorable, a ritual that could be repeated by other lovers ever after. That's how she explained it to the old goldsmith, who understood, for he too was a bit of a metaphysician, or at least he so regarded himself, and besides, he rather liked the lady.

She instructed Benjamin to make the necessary adjustments in the length of the chain and to deliver the pendant to her at the court that evening, because she wanted to be seen wearing it at the ball. The goldsmith eagerly agreed, knowing that now, in the covetous eyes of his neighbors, he would be redeemed for having kept his shop open on Santa Martina's Day, for had not the Princess Maria de Caravajal y Moroto validated the legitimacy of his independence, his pragmatism and reasonableness, and his loyalty to his Jewish heritage and law, by not only doing business with him on this day but also inviting him to the palace to complete that business? Chuckling to himself, he knew that next year on Santa Martina's Day there would not be a Jew in the city who would close his shop, and every one of them would self-righteously proclaim that he was obeying a law higher than any the Bishop could impose. There might even be a few converts to the practice from among the Gentiles, he smiled.

And here the tale ends—or rather, here Mosseh Alvares' tale ends. As noted, there were other, more elaborate versions that later showed up, several of them popular with Christian audiences, as a matter of fact. Presumably, if they were moral tales, they held a slightly different moral than did Alvares' tale, for his, it will be remembered, was told to his daughter, Rachel, who, having endured a lustful glance from the abbot, Bernardo de Balbuena, had been moved to rage and a desire for revenge, a desire her father thought both improper and injudicious to satisfy.

One wonders what the Puritan might have made of this parable. In the past, surely he would have seen through its flimsy fabric of rationalizations and pragmatism, and of course he never would have been particularly moved by the plights of the several characters, the Duke, the heartbroken girl (for that is how all versions leave her, heartbroken, deserted by her lover for another woman who is wealthy, beautiful, innocent even), and the aged Jewish artisan who must adjust his life to the terms decreed by a population so much larger than he that it seemed to him like Fate and his maneuvers like designs to outwit Fate. The Puritan would have calculated each character's unit value and measured the total against a universal moral scale, converting those units and measures into an algebra, a moral equation that he would try to apply to his own life. He would fail in this attempt, of course; or the equation, the tale, would fail; and, once again, he would be left staring into the blizzard-like whiteness of his self, longing for transformation, dying for redemption, stumbling in his pain against madness and sometimes even holding himself there, momentarily mistaking it for transcendence.

But that was long ago, or at least it was before the beginning of this particular tale, and now the Puritan has at last wobbled upon his Arctic-facing pivot and has let his eyes fall elsewhere, here, for instance, upon the poor old Jewish exile in the Caribbean whiling away his idle afternoon and his daughter's rage by telling her a tale that casts him in a role he has imagined will save them both. Or else the Puritan has let his gaze fall upon the abbot himself, Bernardo de Balbuena, and his epic poem, *El Bernardo,* a marvel of ingenuity and diligence, a poem that to most readers has seemed sadly beneath the author's ambitions for it, which were, as indicated by his correspondence as much as by the text itself, to have it serve as a national epic, with El Bernardo himself ascending to take a seat in the pantheon of national heroes beside the deathless figures of Roland, Arthur, Aeneas, and Ulysses.

The poem is maze-like in structure, or better, is a maze within a maze, in which the object is not so much to find one's way out as it is to find one's way in. But since Balbuena's immediate purpose, if indeed it was to let the reader into his poem and thus into the interior zones of his life, was somewhat different from the purpose behind this tale, was in fact precisely opposite it, then it would seem legitimate, if not imperative, that one provide as brief and simple a summary of the action as possible. What follows, then, is the merest outline. The author is indebted to John Van Horne for the structure of his summary. As the reader will immediately perceive, the difficulties of describing simply the plot line of Balbuena's epic are many. The poem is in twenty-four books of forty-four thousand lines of eleven syllables each in eight-line stanzas, rhyming A-A-B-B-C-C-B-A, with an allegorical commentary in prose at the end of each book, plus "The Prologue," written, as mentioned, while Balbuena was in residence in Villa de la Vega (doubtless the reason, incidentally, why a copy of the first edition of *El Bernardo* is exhibited today in the West Indies Research Library in Kingston, where it is labeled "The First Book Published by a Resident of Jamaica"). Nevertheless, despite the difficulties, here is a summary of *El Bernardo*.

The hero, after a love affair between the Count of Saldaña and the King's sister, is born.[4] The King imprisons the Count and thrusts his sister into a convent, whereupon the boy, Bernardo, is singled out by the fairies, who, in the system of marvels employed by the poet to explain the workings of the world, control most of the world's physics. The fairies have chosen the child to become their instrument of destruction against France, and, to that end, he is placed into the care of Orontes, a wise man and magician, to be educated and reared. He is taught all the knightly virtues and all the arts of war, for it has

---

[4] It seems pointless to indicate each of the literally hundreds of facts and events common to the biographies of both El Bernardo, epic hero, and his creator, the Abbot of Jamaica, except to note that, indeed, there are hundreds of them and that the hero's illegitimate birth is but the first, unless, of course, one wishes to count the identity of their given names, Bernardo, as the first.

been determined in conference between the fairies and Orontes that
Bernardo will end up killing the powerful Roland and destroying the
entire French army at Roncesvalles. But before he can do this, he
must first prove himself in a succession of adventures. As an
unknown young man he saves his uncle, King Alfonso, from an am-
bush. An invisible power then guides him to a boat. He embarks,
and the boat soon meets with a ship, aboard which are the King of
Persia and Angelica, a Princess of Cathay. The King of Persia dubs
Bernardo a knight. Then, to free Angelica, Bernardo fights and
wounds the King and afterwards helps to cure him. On an island he
sees a lovely woman rising from the sea in a pearl-encrusted chariot.
On shore the chariot changes into a doe with golden horns. Bernardo follows it into the forest and comes to a cave, where he sees the
ubiquitous Angelica in the arms of a serpent, which, spying Bernardo, flees deeper into the cave. Bernardo follows and comes out in
a meadow where he sees two giants, one of which has killed the serpent, while the other drags Angelica off by the hair. Bernardo pur-
sues them. One giant squares off against Bernardo with a mace.
They fight, but wherever Bernardo wounds him wasps, instead of
blood, spurt from the wound. When Bernardo strikes at the wasps,
they change into gold coins. Finally, Bernardo cuts the giant in two.
The lower half sinks to the ground in the form of a puddle of blood,
the upper half flies off into the air. Bernardo, without singeing a
hair, chases the second giant into a wall of flame. A spirit then con-
ducts him to a boat that cuts through the dark water thick with ser-
pents. At daybreak, he finds himself in bed in a hall filled with various treasures. He gets out of bed, leaves the hall, and comes upon
two castles, one of Youth and Beauty, the other of Aged Ugliness.
Aged Ugliness attacks Youth and Beauty, which defends itself with
roses. Bernardo sees Angelica at the window of the castle of Youth
and Beauty and tries to rescue her. Evil spirits attack him, but he
captures one who, in exchange for her freedom, tells him how to
catch and bind Proteus, who is known for his ability to change into
many shapes. Proteus appears, and they meet in pitched battle. Proteus fights valiantly, but Bernardo holds him fast. Finally, caught in
pearl chains, Proteus gives up and tells Bernardo what he wants to

know, i.e., who his parents are, what his ancestry is, and what vic-
tories will he win in the future. Proteus now disappears, and Bernardo finds himself clad in Achilles' armor. Entering a garden, he is
welcomed by two beautiful female forms who tell him that the armor
had been preserved for him and that he is now in Alcina's garden.
After this, in a series of adventures fighting pirates at sea, he joins
forces with the King of Persia to try to rescue Angelica. He goes to
the aid of some hapless maidens who have been taken to Crete as
human sacrifices, and there he meets and falls in love with Arcangelica, the daughter of Angelica and Mars, the god of war. Arcangelica is dressed in a knight's armor and has come to Crete to attempt to rescue her mother. She falls in love with Bernardo. They
are parted, and he goes in search of her. He is cast ashore on an island where, on the banks of a river, stands the Castle of Themis, the
goddess of law, wisdom, and equity. He enters the castle and sees
two women, one lascivious, the other, who is the goddess Themis
herself, virtuous and wise. Men in the shapes of hairy beasts keep
appearing from a fountain, and most of them choose the lascivious
one. A few, though, through good fortune rather than deliberate
intent, stumble across the floor to Themis, drink from the cup she
proffers, and are changed from beasts back into men. Themis tells
Bernardo that her cup holds all the intelligence in the world. The
other cup, she tells him, holds ignorance and deceit. Bernardo
chooses to follow the way of Themis, is given light by her, and thus
he now wears both the armor of Achilles and the wisdom of Themis.
He leaves her and, after first defeating all the forces of ignorance ar-
rayed on the slopes of Mount Parnassus, climbs to the top, where he
meets Apollo, who predicts that a poet, i.e., Balbuena himself, will
sing Bernardo's fame. Illuminated by wisdom and the knowledge of
his coming fame, Bernardo returns to his true destiny, Spain, and
the coming fight with France. But first, at the mouth of the Ebro
River, he meets a dragon with a wide mouth, wide enough, in fact,
to swallow him whole. In the dragon's stomach, Bernardo has many
adventures. He meets and fights with a giant Moor. Wounding the
Moor, he draws blood, of course, but, instead of blood, gold coins
tumble out. Then, from each coin that falls, there springs an arm

with a sword. A maiden, who seems at home in the dragon's stomach, is seated close by, holding the magic sword of Achilles, the one piece of essential equipment that Bernardo has so far been unable to obtain. But the giant Moor grabs up Achilles' sword and wounds Bernardo in the side. Bernardo fights back bravely. The giant dissolves into thin air, and Bernardo suddenly finds himself in a palace beside a beautiful lady, Iberia. In the palace is a fountain from which every man can obtain whatever he most desires. Bernardo's choice is Fame. The sword of Achilles, wet with Bernardo's own blood, is now his to keep, for it had been imperfect until plunged into royal blood, in this case, his own. All the adventures of Bernardo previously related are now revealed to have been leading up to his obtaining this sword and his being prepared by his many tests to undergo the ordeals of a hero, to make the right choices and respond properly to the challenges offered by other heroes, in particular the French hero Roland. Iberia explains to him the great Spanish names and lineages that are woven on the tapestries on the walls. Among the lineages there is a description of the line of the family of the prophesied poet, Balbuena. Famous now, and armed with a sword that can cut through all the enchanted armor of Roland, Bernardo sallies out and proceeds to have his first encounter with the French hero, who, in the meantime, has been going through a set of adventures and tests curiously like Bernardo's, except that Roland's have been without the same purposeful sense of destiny as Bernardo's. In this first encounter with Roland, Bernardo unhorses the great paladin, who is dazed by the agony of defeat. Bernardo is thrilled by his victory. It is but a preview of their encounter at Roncesvalles, however. In the meanwhile, Bernardo reaches the climax of his series of adventures with his entry into the enchanted Castle of Carpio. He is told that his missing love, Arcangelica, has entered the castle. Declaring that all enchantments can be conquered by a determined knight, Bernardo enters the castle amidst flames and with the earth quaking. He does not see Arcangelica, but he is attacked by a bull, which he fights. They fall into a pit of water, and Bernardo loses consciousness. He awakens to find himself embracing a beautiful woman who tells him that the magician Clemesi from Africa, of the

Carpio family, was buried here by Hercules, that he built this castle himself and installed in it a magic mirror in which the future can be seen. Bernardo looks into the mirror and sees that he is not destined to marry Angelica or Arcangelica, but instead a Princess Crisalba, whose hand he'd won at a joust in Acaya but had left to follow Arcangelica, who, dressed in knight's armor, had jousted evenly with him. Now it's decreed by destiny that he is to forget these others and marry Crisalba, suitably a Christian lady. From this union will spring a succession of famous families, chief among them the Castro family, which will produce the much praised Count Lemos, President of the Council on the Indies. Having thus accepted his destiny once and for all, the beautiful woman, the magic mirror, the wall of flames, all the music, and other apparatus rapidly disappear, and Bernardo now finds himself the owner of the very real and unenchanted Castle of Carpio. Inside the castle, he finds Orontes, his wise old teacher, together with three hundred armed knights. With these he leaves for León, to ask royal pardon for his father, who has been in prison all these intervening years. He joins the King, who is on his way to meet the attacking French army at Roncesvalles in the Pyrenees. After many omens predicting French defeat, the battle is fought. Bernardo and Roland at last meet in a truly prodigious battle. Bernardo, helped by his destiny, wins, and here the poem ends.

For clarity's sake, what has been left out are the various adventures of Roland which parallel those of Bernardo; also the tales of Ferragut, the Spanish Moor, who, having been told of the fame of Bernardo and the glory he will eventually acquire, burns to emulate him but gets himself inadvertently tangled up with the enchantress Arleta, who, once embraced, becomes an old hag. Also omitted are the adventures of the noble Goths, Teudonio and Gundémaro; of Morgante, King of Corsica; the adventures of the tricky Garilo; the conferences of the French king at court; the innumerable tales that the various characters tell; the saintly miracles; and the conversion of the Moors to Christianity. Also the discovery of the eighth-century King Rodrigo of Spain, still doing penance one hundred years later for having lost Spain to the Arabs through his seduction of a young Arab girl; and the story of Estordián, who turns into a silkworm,

and of his lover, who, weeping for him, turns into a fountain. Also
the battles, duels, clashes, and enchantments of Malgesí, the French
enchanter; of the Dutch Arnold of Espurg, who owns the magic ring
of Angelica with which he turns Garilo into a cat; of the Tlaxcalan
magician of Mexico, who conjures down from the air the flying boat
of Malgesí in which the latter and two companions, the King of
Persia and Reinaldos, have already taken a trip to the moon and are
now viewing the as yet undiscovered New World. Also omitted is the
Tlaxcalan's prediction of the events of the New World, in which
Jamaica, as the future abbotship of the prophesied poet, Balbuena,
comes at last into its epic destiny!

The Puritan smiles. If nothing more had come down to the present time and place from the lives of Bernardo de Balbuena and
Mosseh Alvares, he observes, than this bizarrely mediocre epic poem
written by the former and the rather shapeless and morose version of
a medieval tale told by the latter, one might miss entirely the point of
their two lives. For instance, one would be free, no, one would be
compelled to disregard the gap that lay between the sheer ordinari-
ness, on the one hand, of Balbuena's life as a Church bureaucrat,
his tedious accumulation of wealth and trivial power, his fawning
courtship of those of high station, and, on the other hand, his life as
that poem, its grandiose literary ambition, the baroquely curling
shape of its hero's biography and his practically genetic integrity.
Thus, reasons the Puritan, by having missed the tactile facticities of
Balbuena's daily life, and also its lifelong patterns, one would have
missed the spark that during his life flew between it and the other
pole, the poem—and, by so doing, one would have missed *everything*. That spark was everything. It's how one forgives oneself and
others.

And the same is true for Alvares. By one's refusal to imagine his
oppressed and depressing daily life, in which the elderly Jew must ignore the local abbot's salacious stares against the body of his only
daughter, a lifetime in which he must grind away his intelligence
and physical force as a humble artisan imprisoned by history in a
colony of exiles located at the end of the known world, a place
where, to inflate his sense of social worth, he must have fantasies

that he alone is responsible for his community's cultural integrity—by one's refusal to imagine that life, the Puritan says to himself, one determines not to perceive how that life makes another, more lucid life possible, and perhaps even necessary. One means, of course, not Benjamin, the "patriarch" of Alvares' tale, but the process that created Benjamin.

The Puritan might therefore see the two of them, Balbuena and Alvares, as puttering away at signs of self that are larger than the self and as coming together, for these few moments, at least, to create yet a third image, a third sign of self that is larger than self. For if the reader now could but see this third putterer, who, bent over his desk late at night, squints and carefully lays down yet another tangled sentence, if the reader could but see that figure a-writing, he'd know how it is that such a peculiar, self-created thing as a new world can exist. And then the reader would see a fourth figure, his own, reading. And on, and on.